I, KINGPIN

WHAT HAPPENS WHEN THEY DON'T GET CAUGHT

P.L. Dates Jr. MB.GH.

PFARRO/MAX®
7543 Old Alexandria Ferry Road
Clinton, Maryland 20735
www.pfarromax.com

ISBN: 978-0-9762482-0-0

Library of Congress Control Number: 2012913116

The characters and events portrayed in this book are fictitious. Any similarity to real persons, living or dead, is coincidental and not intended by the author or publisher.

Printed in the United States of America

Book Design by TWASolutions.com

ACKNOWLEDGMENTS

To all who read this I want to say Thank You. From my heart I say this. This is my first effort that has been released to the public. There are to date, six other novels to be released. The topics are different and diverse.

Although many of my friends are no longer here physically in spiritual essence, they are here.

My father always believed in me, even we he stood alone, for that I dedicate this first effort to him also to Vernon Dobyns (Beaver) my first cousin who was more of an older brother and as well the light of my formative years.

This novel's topics go from brutal to vulgar at times comical, also sexual. In order to be honest to this lifestyle and its truths, it was necessary to include certain expletives. For those who have lived this life or been very close it, any other effort would have been insulting to you the reader. Life is not a sterile kitchen; I refuse to accommodate or acquiesce to the squeamish in picturing it.

I would also like to thank Tiffany Sampson for her help and confidence in the project, even in the very outset. There were many others who assisted and believed in this effort, to you all I say...

Thank You.

P.L.Dates Jr. MB.GH.

I, KINGPIN

Preface

Man, listen!

Before we get this thing started I want you to understand that being a KINGPIN is not by any means an easy achievement. That's right, I said achievement. For those of you who question this statement, you go and try that shit and then come and talk to me.

First off, you should understand something about what a Kingpin is. Merriam Webster's Collegiate Dictionary defines it in two ways. The first is: The pin that stands in the middle of a triangular arrangement of bowling pins. I think the more befitting definition for this reading is the second one, which states: *The chief person in a group or undertaking*. Even this standard description does not fully comprise the Kingpin you will shortly be reading about. The Kingpin illustrated in these pages is an individual who must be many things, to many people.

This chronicle will be, to say the least, a modern day look at what an everyday black street Kingpin encounters. I hate to use comparisons, especially when speaking of my own work, but if I had to, I would call this a written account something akin to the HBO series, "The Sopranos."

I mean this in the sense that "The Sopranos" has provided the average American a glimpse of what an Italian Mafia "BOSS" faces on a day to day basis. More precisely, the ups and downs of criminal enterprise that most rappers know little about, even as they consistently glamorize these individuals and their lifestyles in their raps. While these lifestyles display a glamorous surface, glamour is ultimately in the eye of the individual.

The typical cautionary tale that you hear involves some criminally-involved gangster/kingpin type who tells his story with great remorse because he is older and wiser, or just sorry as hell that he got caught. Currently rotting behind the force of inescapable steel bars, of course *he* speaks with remorse: For he has little choice. Such, however, is not the case in the chronicle you will shortly encounter. The question (or shall I say situation that never gets answered or addressed) is: What happens to the so-called gangster who doesn't get caught? What happens after the gunfight, after the smoke clears? After the Feds comb the area, unable to locate the prized suspect? Or, finally, what happens when our criminal doesn't turn states witness and doesn't die in a blaze of gun-fire or glory, but must instead continue trudging onward?

Ask your average elder, 'what happens to the really tough, rebellious, bad-ass motherfuckers in the neighborhood?' They will almost automatically tell you that these types wind up either dead or in jail. That, more or less, is the general consensus about the bad guy rebel. It seems, perhaps, more soothing to the human spirit to warn kids that the bad guys always get it in the end. *Comeuppance* awaits him. *Karma* will track him down. *Live by the sword, die by the sword.*

While such sentiments might warm your heart, does this necessarily mean they reflect the full extent of truth?

Or could it be that the Kingpin lives next door? Is he the butcher at the local Safeway? Or maybe he's the trucker that just delivered your dining room furniture? Or possibly the non-bonded plumber who charges a little cheaper than most? Nah☐couldn't be. The Kingpin is dead or in jail.

Or is he?

In the Beginning

The years that crack came into development on the streets of Brooklyn, I was there. I remember the large amount of crews and individuals who became millionaires from their dealings with this new irresistible product. I was but a fledgling criminal at this time. I had a small crew of young guys who were equally as hungry to get to the top of New York's crime ladder. All the while, I'd listened to many of the old school crooks and learned a lot about the rules of the ghetto. Admittedly, many of them had by now faded into neighborhood drunks and derelicts. Their fate, I would learn, was largely brought about by a string of bad decisions, time and time again. While the info I extracted from these old-timers cost me no more than a fifth of liquor or a three-dollar vile of crack, over time their insights proved to be priceless.

The average person views one's current situation as permanent, seeing only the present tense. They figure today a bum, yesterday a bum and that you-always-were-and-will-be-a- bum. To be honest, I was always intrigued by the various feats many of these men had pulled-off in life, even if they currently had little left to show for. Today or yesterday, I felt that their accomplishments were immense simply because they'd been accomplished.

Now don't go thinking I took any old thing they said at their word. I would cross-reference and fact-check my bums' various accounts based on their ages, and the particular section of town they cited. I would check out their stories with other people unrelated to them. I mean, let's face it, though these motherfuckers were once on top of the game, today they brought up the rear. So you never knew what was what unless you did your homework. And doing my homework like a dedicated student gave me a history of what went down before the current state. It also schooled me on the happenings of other drug lords and street legends who had come and gone. I quickly learned how knowing the past of a situation better prepared you to deal with the current or future state of things. Sooner than later, this wisdom would propel my desire to make moves of my own.

The team I put together was really odd unit. First off, my man Rasheed Strings was quite the character. Fair-skinned with wavy grains of hair, he also had a chip on his shoulder about the shit. He had gone to jail early on in life. I mean as barely a teen, Ra was in and out the joint. He felt that people in jail always sought to hold your good looks against you. Or at least they held his against him. As Ra saw it, since he was always assumed to be the bitch, he would stab one or two motherfuckers, right off the bat, just to establish that he was no bitch, despite what they thought they saw on the surface.

Ra always stayed in real good shape. Originally into acrobatics, he could do back handsprings all the way down a city block with no problem. His hands were fast and he had a real physical ability. His quick temper was often a problem early on but as time went on he did mellow out some. I recall a few times there were missions I thought should be better brainstormed before diving into head-first. My gut always told me not to participate until the background work was done. Yet, Ra went on and did the damn deed without me. I also remember visiting him in jail on an early occasion or two behind a busted mission that simply needed a little more thought and planning to have succeeded.

I was with doing the essentials of what needed to be done, but I realized that Ra was a bit of a thrill seeker. That's where we differed. I, as well, was all for the thrill: but thrill for profit. Certainly not thrill for thrill's sake.

Incredibly, Ra and I were the same height, same build, both fairly nice-looking young guys. If a honey didn't like one, it was sure that she would like the other. Or more often than not, she dug us both. Ra was an incredible mathematician. He very seldom ever wrote any numbers down. Say he met a female on Tuesday, he'd hear her recite her phone number one time and remember it well throughout the weekend. The thing that killed me about the shit was that he expected me to be able to this as well. I was better than most with remembering things. I did pretty well but there was no way that I was going to keep up with Ra. It wasn't just remembering numbers it was adding, subtracting, multiplying and calculating. Damn near anything that you could do with numbers, he did it. I really feel he had a gift.

The only thing that Ra and I had real conflict and damn near hostile disagreements about was him getting high. He didn't use crack or anything but he kept an itch for some weed or PCP. This cat seemed to get some kind of kick out of fighting while he was high. I'm not sure if it was his true personality coming through, or the lack of inhibitions that the high feeling gave him. He didn't care if it was one on one or not. Even when the odds, were obviously against him; Ra loved to get high and fight.

"There is no way to fight fair." That was Ra's famous philosophy. He would get on that PCP and take all of his clothes off and threaten groups of niggas. I was with his ass a couple of times when we were just hanging out. Out the blue, this motherfucker wants to slap the shit out of some guy in a nightclub. Me being

13

young and strong, what the fuck, I didn't mind a good fight and all. But if I'm your man, at least let me know you were going to set some shit off like that.

"Damn Ra, I just ordered a drink from the bar. That's good money I wasted."

"Nigga what did you want me to do, send you a smoke signal?" was Ra's response. "I told you to always be prepared for anything, anyway."

That's the type of shit I'm talking about. Ra for the most part was one of the smartest people I'd ever known. How he applied his knowledge didn't always match the amount of knowledge that he had.

He and I viewed each other as equals but he knew that he had a bad temper so he kind of let it be known that I was the main man. Not to mention the fact that he knew that I had been preparing for being the main man -- better yet, the "Kingpin" -- for a lifetime. Ra said many times before, "Nigga you love some 'clieca' " (another word for big crew or gang).

Ra's thought was, "fuck a whole group of anything." He'd prefer it be just him and me against the odds. "I think we can do it," Ra would always say. "Why let all these chumps get paid along with us?"

Ace is High

Austintine Havolice (street-name, 'Ace') is the 'Young Bleed'. I had a connection to this kid that was uncanny. Ace was a perpetual hot-head when we first met. I don't know what it was about me and hot-heads, but they sure stayed on my radar.

He came up on me in the street and was thirsty. I had seen that thirsty, 'wanna-to-be-rich' look before. He had enough sense to know that we were really getting paid. And he wanted in. I respected the fact that he wanted in, but that he didn't act pressed. When I say didn't act pressed, I mean he wanted in but he didn't whine, act like a bitch or try to kiss our asses (at least not too much).

"Look I've got my own two guns and I'm willing to use these motherfuckers on anybody you say! Anytime you say! So what's up?" he asked, before quickly continuing: "I know how to cook coke, cut dope and mix PCP. I don't know very much about

15

'pimpin', but the bitches love me and I'm willing to find out how to turn that love into money. I know you guys have a closed crew, but I'm even willing to buy my way in. I've got two grand and I'll put all of it up to show you I'm down. I ain't got no place I've got to be and no place to go. I'll flow with you cats as long as it takes. But I ain't nobody's bit-."

Before he could get the rest of the word out his mouth, I had pulled my pistol and pressed it against his right eye.

I told him that Ra would ask him some questions and he had less than five seconds to answer each one. If he stuttered or hesitated he would have all of eternity to figure out what went wrong.

"Bitch ass nigga how you find out about us?" was Ra's first question.

"Swanson, the muscle bound derelict, said that Briscoe would probably be the next big-time nigga to do big things around here. Based on the way he thinks and that you were his man."

"Swanson...," thought Ra out loud, "Remind me to knock another tooth out his mouth when I see him again B. He runs his mouth too much." Ra turned his attention back to the kid Ace.

"You come running up in our faces, talking about you want to roll with the likes of us, based on what the fuck some known pipehead told you!" Ra was building up steam. "You know how far me and the God go back! You ain't prepared to run with us, ya bitch! This is real life! This ain't no movie! Where is this two grand that you say you've got?"

"I ain't gonna tell your ass, Ra," cried the kid. "You'll probably rob my ass for it."

"Well," I said, still sizing the kid, "you said you was gonna give it to us anyway. Plus when you deal with him you deal with me." I pulled the hammer back on my pistol. "Now where's the money?"

"It's in my nut-sack."

"No problem," Said Ra. He pulled the kids belt and pants away from his stomach. Reached down in the kid's pants and grabbed the dough wad. "Yea it looks like about two g's to me."

I glanced at Ace.

"You know how many young shorties want to get with this crew?" I told him that if he could get one thousand dollars up in two days I would consider his application.

"I don't care how much small change you come up with," Ra interrupted, "you won't run with this squad, cause you're a bitch! You didn't even put up a struggle when I took your dough."

"I had a gun in my eyeball motherfucker! What did you want me to do?"

"Look, shut the fuck up," I told him.

"I've held your balls bitch," Ra added. "I don't care what you ever do. You'll always be a ho-ass kid to me!"

17

I told Ace to get the fuck out of here and I would send for him when I wanted to see him.

"How you gonna know where I'm at? I told you, I'm basically homeless!"

"Yeah, and I said I'll send for you when I need to see you. And by the way, give those pistols of yours to Ra."

As Ace rolled out, relieving himself of his weapons, I'm sure he was scared as shit. But he left with a purposeful look on his face that left little trace.

I asked Ra what he thought of the kid?

"Fuck that little piece of shit," blurted Ra. "Let's go down to the 'Greens' and spend his little bit of money up in case it's marked." The Greens being the street name for the legendary "Tavern on the Greens." This is a place where the affluent often go to chill. If not there, we might have gone to the Shark Bar. We were not supposed to be in most of those places ourselves but, every now and then we would go and spend a little dough. Just to show we had some juice.

"Come on Ra! Seriously," I asked again. "What do you think of this kid?"

"I told you I think he is a little runaway bitch who ain't never gonna be shit! Man, don't tell me that you've taken some kind of liking to this little shit?"

"I'm saying, come on, he had to have a lot of balls to even come up to us at all with that shit."

"Yeah, but it don't cut no ice with me. He - is - still - a - BITCH!"

"Now Ra, why are you saying that? We've robbed grown motherfuckers who didn't handle having a gun in their face as well as that kid did."

"Well, I grabbed his balls and his money and he didn't do shit".

"Well, other than farting on your hand what did you want him to do? I had a 45 in his face."

"Whatever! I would have had more respect for him if he had farted on my knuckles".

"Yeah, and then what would you have done?"

"I would have killed that piece of shit right there on the spot!"

"Exactly. That's why he didn't do it."

"Yeah, he would have been dead, but I would have respected his ass".

"Look, I say we give the kid a couple of days and then I'll send for him. If he has the dough we let him in on a trial basis."

"Fuck that piece of shit. If you want him in, it's cool with me. But let it be known he goes down as your man."

"Alright that's the deal."

"Look, I don't particularly care about this kid in one way or the other. But, if it gets out that this kid got down by running up to the two of us in the street and applying, we won't be able to make a move without every runaway for five blocks coming up asking, 'How can I be down'? Right now we don't need that type of attention or any kind of attention for that matter. You feel me?"

I agreed all the way, but as long as Ace had the money when I sent for him, he was in.

The Interview

About a week had gone by and I'm sure Ra had forgotten all about that kid Ace. Ace didn't think that I saw him but I did. He was coming up the block from the bodega we often frequented. Again, this little fucker comes up to one of my crew, anxious and eager.

"What's up with you contacting me?" My young Sergeant quickly hit him in the gut before asking, "Ra who is this clown?"

"What is your name again kid 'shit stain', no, no, 'Seamore' " Ra could barely get it out for the laughter. I remember thinking that I hadn't seen Ra laugh like that in front of other people in a long time. I gestured to bring the kid downstairs to the stock room. Ra stopped laughing quickly and so did the others. The kid was just starting to get his breath back.

In the midst of all this foolishness I noticed that the kid had on the same clothes that he had on the day we first spoke. There were about five of my associates in that room. As he began to come to, he was greeted with one of Ra's nasty looks. "I told you he was a bitch and would never be shit but a bitch".

I instructed two of my young sergeant's to begin. They tied him up and began whipping his ass. Before they started, Ace said, "You never sent for me."

"I told you I would send for you when I was ready to see you", I briefly replied.

The beating began and after about 15 minutes, Ra and myself, went upstairs to go get something to eat. Two Days later, Ace came out of what could be described as a mild coma-like state. He was greeted and had been getting taken care of by an attractive young lady. "Where the fuck am I?" was his first question.

"You are in your apartment," she calmly replied.

"But I don't have no fucking apartment."

"Oh yes you do."

"I remember being in the basement of this bodega getting my ass kicked by a few of Briscoe's soldiers. I thought sure I was gonna be killed."

"You don' know how close you came to getting put in just that condition."

"I got to get to talk to Briscoe just one more time. I got to get into his crew."

"Relax. Your ass won't be going any were for at least a week. You are dehydrated; you've got several badly bruised ribs and a slight concussion. Not to mention, you have lost quite a bit of blood and your bandages will need changing."

"How the fuck do you know all that shit?"

"I was here when the doctor got through examining your ass."

"Doctor!? Wait a minute. How long have I been in this joint?"

"Let's see. About three days, if you include the first night that you were brought in."

"Wait a motherfucking minute! Somebody carried me in here?"

"Yeah, you would not have been able to crawl in here for all the money in Trump Towers."

"I've got to take the thousand that I had to Brisco. I've got to get in this crew." The fine young girl pushed him back onto his back.

"Relax Young Bleed, you're in."

"What do you mean I'm in? They fucked me up!"

"That's right. They also took the thousand that you had stashed in that sandwich bag around the corner. But you're in now."

"How'd they know where I had the money stashed?"

"They knew. You thought you were going to be able to surprise those guys? You obviously don't know the clout and contacts this crew has. They could probably tell you how many terds you're gonna shit in the next week."

"So you mean, they gave me this apartment?"

"No. They didn't give it to you, but you can stay here. Let me rephrase that. You will stay here!"

"And what about you? Are you part of the fringe benefits too?"

"I don't think so young bleed. I'm not for you. I'm here to take care of you until you get back on your feet. After that, you're on your own. And stop watching so many damn movies! I guess you think I'm supposed to suck your little dick while you heal up, right?"

"Little dick! I've got your little dick hanging low."

"Yeah right, you forget I told you I was in here when the doctor examined you. I didn't see nothin' but a whole lot of cheap homemade-tattoos on your little ass, oh; and my boyfriend's handy work and knuckle prints on your ribs."

"I don't even remember the guys who were actually hitting me."

"See. That's the kind of stuff I'm talking about Young Bleed. You don't pay enough attention to detail. If you want to make it in this crew, your shit had better get sharp fast!"

"Hey wait a minute what's all this 'Young Bleed' shit."

"Oh that's your name."

"What do you mean? My name is ACE!"

"Well they named you while you were still on the floor. Actually it was Ra that named you. He was laughing and said, 'look how much this young motherfucker bleeds. That's it! I'm gonna call this kid Young Bleed'. Some of the crew liked it and that was it: You are now Young Bleed."

"Damn."

"You'll have to earn the right to be called Ace. Who would want to be called Ace anyway? That shit is corny, some fucking card in a deck? I think Young Bleed is kind of cute."

"Fuck that! My name is Ace and that's what you're gonna call me."

"Take your hand off of my wrist". With a dagger in her other hand that was now underneath his chin.

"My father's name was Ace and he's dead."

"Your gonna be joining him in just a second if you don't take your hand off of me 'YOUNG BLEED.' I don't think you really understand what you've gotten yourself into. This is an organization. However loosely run it may appear to the outsider, it is a very small tight ship. Your ass ain't shit but a deck hand. If you don't like it, you can walk the plank. You better get used to taking orders and liking it. Ain't nobody got no time for no arrogant ass kid who won't do right. I'm gonna give you this one tip. If it wasn't for Brisco himself taking a liking to you, your ass would be dead. And it can still happen. Even though he likes you,

Ra is his man all the way to the grave. Don't think you got no juice just 'cause you got a pass on death."

"Alright, miss-thang. You gonna give me my fucking crime family orientation, are you? I know that I dropped out of school and everything but as I remember the teachers used to write their names on the blackboard. I don't see you writing your name up anywhere."

Silence. Dead and cold-- silence came over the room.

"Hey, bitch! What the hell is your name? You're gonna call me Young Bleed and all that shit but your not gonna tell me your name."

"My name is C.C. call me bitch again and you won't call nobody else one"

"Oh! That's creative. No, what's your real name?"

"I told you my name was C.C. and that's what you'll be calling me. You call me anything else and you'll wish you hadn't."

Now C.C. was a real different character. She was one of the three women that I had on staff. For some reasons that I do understand most of the men in my organization did not really care for her. They may have thought that she was nice-looking or whatever but they really didn't go much further then that with their interest in her. C.C. was very attractive. She liked hyper-activity. She rode motorcycles, jet-ski's and go-carts. She shot a pretty good game of nine-ball. She enjoyed karate and basketball. As far as I know she was not a freak but did enjoy a casual fuck, as long as it was long and good. I did hear a rumor that she made one kid stop and get up in the middle of sex. The rumor goes that as he got out of bed she stabbed him in the butt for wasting her time.

Her former job was a butcher. She was a meat cutter or something for some small grocery chain. They say that she got fired for stealing or threatening the boss or something. I know that her current job for me was a collector. C.C. did hair during the day on Thursday, Friday and Saturdays. To my knowledge, those were the only days that she worked. Being a collector was interesting work. It was something like being a bounty hunter for criminals. I'd say C.C. also had a nice good figure. Well, good enough to fuck. She wasn't a model or nothing but most niggas would fuck her; if they could? She said all the time that she would love to find a man that would fuck the shit out of her and then clip her up when she walked down the street. She said it would be better than having some clown fall in love with her just because of some good sex. She said if a nigga fucked real good and didn't call her she would probably call him.

As far as I was concerned she had a purpose and she served it. If an individual owed the company money my first action would probably be to call C.C. I would tell her where the certain person would hang out and she would somehow get them to ask to go out with her and then she would get them to pay the money back. Most of the time she would just rob them; or get them to show her where their money was.

Of course there was a penalty for being in debt to us. I would usually instruct C.C. to cut something small off of the person. A finger-end, possibly a toe. But on more that one occasion, C.C. had gone too damn far. I had a guy that owed us about $500 plus the VIG. For the most part, I only assigned C.C. to small accounts, usually first time customers. Anyway, C.C. found the guy, took him out on a date and then fucked him. I had told her to punish him with the usual. She took it upon herself to cut off one of the man's testicles. When asked why she did it, she didn't stutter: "Look, he still has one nut left...He's alright. He couldn't do nothing with the two nuts he had no way. The shit might be an improvement!"

I think that's one of the reasons many of the crew didn't like her. I personally didn't have a problem with C.C. Don't know for sure, but I think Ra may have fucked her once. Who knows?

To the Bricks

C.C. had told Ace right. For the most part, my crew was rather small. The thing that set us apart from other organized groups was that we were into different things, or as Wall Street would say, we were diversified. I even had my hands in some of the strip club action, which was bringing us in some pretty good money. It wasn't enough according to Ra. But I let him know that at least it was steady.

"It's penny Annie", Ra said. "A few hundred here and there. Who needs that shit? Plus, you've got to deal with that old bitch Pam."

"Look, it's not your problem. As long as it brings in a profit, why do you care?"

Ra was pissed. He really didn't like the whole thing about the women and money. Time and time again he'd say, "women ain't qualified to do nothing but transport drugs, hold some pistols and spend someone else's money cause they won't get shit from me."

Pam was a Madam that I had run the girls. We had seven apartments throughout the city. Ra and I also had two houses we rented out in Long Island. The job of Pam's girls was to turn a profit each month. We gave her ten thousand per month and it was her job to turn it into twenty or twenty-five grand each month.

The girls, some whores and some strippers, were on staff to generate profits. Pam set their schedule up so that they were responsible for keeping each one of those apartments perfectly clean, at all times. Usually they had two days a week off. One of those days they would clean an apartment and the other day and a half was theirs. There was one or two times that she tried to hold back on the money and say that they were short but you know that I wasn't having that shit. I made her come up with that shit immediately!

There was a lot of jealously out there on the bricks against me and Ra. We were just a little more than some shorties ourselves. We had come a long way in a fairly short period of time. Our crew had size but no one knew exactly how large or small it was. Most people had no idea how far we had gone with this hustling thing.

Ra was no fool and neither was I. Even though he acted like he was un-supportive of the ho's and the brothel, he knew that the shit was steady dough. His pet project was stick-ups. I didn't see the need to continue to do that shit. True, it had presented a lot of seed money in the beginning, but by now we had enough to reinvest in other things without that. I was really ready to leave that shit alone. I could not just put a complete stop to it though.

Ra and I were partners. We didn't call any shots without the other one knowing about it. And for the most part, we agreed and discussed it. The cohesion between he and I, was what made the whole operation work. It was so well understood that there was no dissention between us. That's why Ra couldn't deny the ho money, and I couldn't deny that the stick up money did help. But my question was, did we need that kind of money? I guess it would be a case of a scrupled criminal.

Ever since the day Ra and I met he has been on the go for some dough. I didn't have time for a whole lot of that wild shit. I was trying to get us established as some cats that was down to make major moves. We're not just some gun happy kids that had no tact, class or ability. The stick-ups that Ra would do always had a touch of vulgarity to them. He would make every body get butt-naked and shit. One time he made all of the women hold the men's dicks and all the men place both of their hands on the women's tits. Talking about, "I want everybody's hands were I can see them!" The shit just got ridiculous.

It was a fact that many of the other lower-classed of the

higher-classed criminals were starting to notice us. I didn't need them black balling us before we ever really got started. You could call it a hoodlum scruple if you want. But the society that we are minor members of does have it's own ethics. If your name got to be known for too much foolishness, other crews would distance themselves from you. Based on the fact that you were perceived as a wild cannon.

When I followed up with Ra about the nudity stunt and shit, he said: "nobody's running out of a joint looking for you when they're trying to find their damn draws." That did make a little sense there. He also added, "victims aren't looking at your face as hard during a robbery if they're concerned about their own nudity." Again, that also made sense. But goddamn, did we really need the extra scratch that bad? I guess the truth was evident since the very beginning. Ra liked fast money and lots of sex. I think that this was his way to get both thrills off at the same time. I wasn't far behind him in his endeavors, but my focus was fixed on growing to the next level.

Something else that was constantly going through my mind was regarding what Swanson, the bum, had told me about one of the older drug lords.

"The day will come that you'll see success on the level that you will not have time to be out on the bricks all the time. When that time comes you will need to keep extra special eyes on the newer members of your group. The ones that were not there in the early days to see you put in the hard work. The first assumption will be that you have not really earned the right to be where you are. If this assumption gets challenged, you will have problems." Keeping that in mind, I continued to run some of the missions with Ra. For one, I didn't want him to think that I was getting soft with the arrival of those soft bills.

My next move was to check on the progress of Young Bleed. It had been brought to my attention that he was somewhat unhappy with his station. In other words, he was finding out just how much real work goes into doing what we were doing. He felt that he would just sit back and get paid. He had to work his corner, make pick-ups and deliveries as well as help Pam occasionally with the girls. It was a fact that, in the beginning, the girls were sexually off limits to him. Being a new member of a crew that was obviously getting it (at least in our area) had it's neighborhood perks. But that wasn't enough for Bleed.

I talked to him and he told me that he felt like a nothing in the crew. I told him that his emotions were telling him the truth. He wasn't shit right now, but the chance for him to advance would come soon. He had no idea that I knew he had made a few minor moves on the side. But I did.

"Yo Bleed, what you up to Friday night?" I asked, innocently enough.

"Nothing Brisco, you got a job for me?"

"No. Maybe you and I could just kick the willie-bo-bo for a few hours? You wit it?" He was pleased, I could tell.

"You know I'm with that shit! Where we going? The Greens, Benihannah's or what?"

"Not sure yet. I'll have to see what hits me at the time."

With a pensive look on his face he asked, "Ra going?"

"Nah, I think he got some skirt to fuck." Bleed looked relieved.

See, for me, that was the problem. He was starting to see Ra as the enforcer and me as merely the brain. This was not good because if he felt like that, I'm sure some others in the crew felt the same way. I say this merely because the truth is, at certain levels of the game, you don't usually have very much respect for the smart guy. But you've got a hell of a lot of respect for the enforcer, a motherfucker you're sure will blow your brains out. I knew that Ra was loud and could be very forceful at times, but the problem was not with Ra being Ra. It had more to do with the consensus that I might not straight give it to a nigga if it was deserved.

Bleed and I went out that night. I downplayed the money aspect a little. We were in a Beamer. It was one that I would push every now and then. This was nowhere near the hottest joint that I had. But it was still flyer than most on the road at the time. We started off by checking out the young lawyer shorty that I knew. She had her cousin there and it was cool for a while. We ate, drank and fucked the shit out of them until about 10:30pm. Then we went to Chaou Liews, to get that good food in a nigga. I don't ever get out in the street for a night without getting some food on my gut. Bleed was loving this shit. This is what he had envisioned the *good life* was supposed to be.

"We supposed to be doing this every night," he told me. "How come you don't come and get a brother more often?"

"For starters, me and Ra do this all the time. You just don't get to because your time hasn't come yet."

"See that's the shit I'm talking about man. Why you always got to mention that guy?"

"Who, Ra?"

"Yeah. It's always got to be about you and him. What about me and you making some moves together? That guy's out-dated. All of those stick-ups he does is crazy. That shit fucks with our credibility. It don't seem like he's on the same path you're on."

"Kissing my ass is not the way to move up in this game," I cautioned the kid. "Neither is knocking the man who, for the most part, is your boss."

"I'm not saying that he's useless or anything, but come-on man! Some of that shit that he be doing is not fucking necessary. I know you see that shit B."

35

I pulled the car over and told Ace that if he said one more word about not liking the way Ra did shit he would be dealt with very harshly.

I broke it down further that he was talking about my partner and I would not allow any dissension in this crew. So he had better keep his small ass opinions to himself or pay for it with his life. I reminded him that few people retire from this business.

"Nigga you letting that MO get the best of you." I told him that so that the mood would not get so serious that the evening couldn't continue. I really wanted to keep his ass talking. What he thought was representative of what the new youth was feeling. That was one of the reasons for this evening. I also wanted to hang out with the kid for a few. I was really having a pretty good time with the kid.

But like I said, we did do plenty of this. It wasn't like this was no new shit. (We were just two cats having a good time.) Secretly, to myself, I was feeling the kid. I was really kind of shocked that the kid had seen so much and had been paying so close attention. I didn't want to let him know it though. I also didn't want him to think that he was seeing a lot of things that I couldn't see. Respect was everything in the position that I was in. This is one of the reasons that Ra didn't want the title 'Kingpin'.

Ra knew that you had to always be on your toes and with him

loving to get high and fuck every skirt that would let him, that was just too much damn work. I told the kid that our management styles may differ, but the goal was still the same.

Young Bleed gave me a long glance. "I've got wild respect for you. But the fact is, you're the reason that the crew exists and does as well as it does. Everybody knows it. And your man Ra, for whatever the reason that he is your man, is in the past. That type of nigga was outdated years ago."

I was pulling up outside the club and I acted like I didn't hear that last statement.

We went in, got the royal treatment and all the 'Big Willie' stuff that goes on at the club. First the club owner greeted us personally and seated us in the VIP section's best seats, which was an extra large booth, slightly elevated above the dance floor, in a semi-secluded area that is the center of attraction. We can see everything that goes on and yet remain untouchable if we chose to. They brought us a couple of bottles of Moet, on the house, because they know we're the biggest tippers in the place. It's somewhat of an investment for them. Secondly, we were also assigned our own personal bartender and waiter for the night. Finally, they sent us the club ho's of our choice. These were girls who frequent the club all the time and basically want to stay around guys who they feel are powerful or paid. They'll do anything you ask because they want the acclaim that comes with being around you. You get special treatment, when you're somebody.

When we were coming out of the club, I noticed this guy giving a pound to Bleed.

"Who was he?" I asked.

"Oh that nigga ain't shit, just a clown I know."

I saw what went on between the two, but again acted as if I didn't. I informed him I'd be picking him up in the morning. When the next day came I had the so-called 'clown' he'd spoken to tied up and sitting in a chair. I picked Young Bleed up and brought him to where the clown was. I told him the next time that he made a dollar that wasn't reported to this crew, he would receive exactly the same treatment that the clown was set to receive.

First the clown was cut with a straight razor in about twenty places. The dude was already naked. I was the one doing the cutting as well as every thing else. There was no one else there but Bleed, the clown and myself. I told Bleed not to take his eyes off of the clown's eyes. I had a spray bottle that was filled with straight rubbing alcohol. I began to spray the man all over. At extremely close range. He was yelling out in excruciating pain. I then took a ball pine hammer and broke both of his knees as well as his ankles. The same hammer was used to break the man's jawbone. First the left side; then the right.

At that point it didn't make much difference because the man had passed out into a state of shock. Some of this beating was because of the remarks that Bleed had made concerning Ra. I didn't let him know that though. The man being unconscious stopped absolutely nothing. Young Bleed had to be taught a lesson about the individuals that he was working for and around.

Bleed had thrown up twice throughout this. I warned him to stop acting like a bitch. I had Bleed stand within two feet, close enough so he could hear the clown shriek in pain and smell him defecate and urinate all over himself. Bleed had made fifty dollars off of his little side venture with the clown. When it was through Bleed was handcuffed to the man for the last few hours of his life. I asked Bleed to explain to the man how it was worth it. Was the clown's life worth the fifty dollars Bleed had made? Was making money behind the backs of the niggas who put him on worth the clown never seeing his friends, family or children again?

"Go ahead Bleed tell him how all of this was worth it!"

As I stood there in front of Bleed, I told him to look into my eyes. He hesitated, forcing me to repeat the command. As he looked into my eyes, there was one slow rolling tear running down his face. He had a look of mixed emotion in his eyes. Part of it looked like fear, some of it looked like pain, and a lot of it looked like a new-found respect mixed with a dash of admiration.

"Who am I nigga?"

"THE KINGPIN," he responded. I was expecting him to say *Brisco* or maybe even *boss*. But I accepted what he said and before I knew it, I had added: "And don't you ever forget it."

KINGPIN had always been the customary name for the position that I held, but had never actually been the name that I'd been called.

Until, of course, that moment.

The KINGPIN

The next few weeks Bleed was forced to create twice the dough of the other crewmembers in similar seniority. Bleed made the amounts and I told him that if he continued that I would consider his application for advancement. I noticed that other members were generating more money as well. All of a sudden everybody was calling me KINGPIN. Everywhere I went bums and store owners who had known me since childhood were not calling me Briscoe, not calling me B, but shouting out 'KINGPIN'.

I got a hold of Ra, figuring that this was his doing. He said he figured it was my doing.

"Even in reference," Ra warned me, "people are referring to you as The Kingpin.

I asked Ra to meet me at the Batcave, a name that he and I used to describe my town house in Long Island. We called his spot the Ranch.

"I'll be there in two hours," Ra informed me.

Before he got to me, I went to go talk to Joe Redds. Joe and I went way back and we had always used each other as confidants when needed. Joe had been through much of the same shit that I had but he was from Philly. Thus, we often had slightly differing views on things, but that was part of the beauty of the shit.

"Yo, Joey what's up it's…"

"…Yeah, *The Kingpin*, I know."

"What! You've herd about that shit too."

"Yeah I got wind of it."

"Yo! How the fuck is this shit getting started Joe?"

"You started it B."

"What do you mean started it?"

"You put that kid on some brand new and he let it be known that you ain't no slouch."

"Wait, a second I wasn't no slouch before."

"Yeah -but the new age motherfuckers wasn't completely convinced. But now without a doubt you and your crew are the airs to the crime thrown, at least in your parts."

"What about Ra?

"They always knew he was a wild-ass nigga. Rumor about that nigga is he shot his brother and his own mother is on the run-from him. Thing is, Ra's known all over for his rowdiness, and the fact that the nigga is hard to kill. But you lay a lot lower. A lot of niggas wasn't sure what you yourself would do. But now the thing is they ain't sure how you might play shit. And that's good."

"Fuck you mean that's good. These new motherfuckers don't define who the fuck I am. I was here before they got here and will be here long after they are dead and stinking!"

"Yo, B, I think you're getting this shit all wrong. I don't think anybody's trippin' because you did what you did. It's the fact that you saw what happened and did nothing that night. Came back the next day and acted like everything was cool and then extracted revenge and respect at the same time. Plus the fact that you didn't fuck up the nigga who for all intense purposes was stealing from the crew, but you put it on an innocent runner. That's the difference between you and Ra. His shit is like straight revenge or malice; your shit's for reason and purpose, which takes more thought. That scares a lot of people because they know that they can't think on your level. That's what makes you The Kingpin. Personally I think the shit was a pure stroke of fucking genius. Most motherfuckers work a lifetime in the streets to get the rep that you have established in one day or shall I say one night. You are right where you need to be right now. But I gotta tell you that right now your ass is Tupac."

I asked him what he meant by that.

"You getting old or something nigga?...It means, all eyes are on you."

"Ok, Ok nigga, you caught me slippin'."

The ride to my rest gave me some time to think about what Joe had said as well as hear my own thoughts. I also had to get ready to hear what Ra was thinking about this whole Kingpin thing. I got to the crib about twenty minutes before Ra did. I blessed him with our usual greeting. As usual, Ra was Ra.

"What the fuck is up my nigga?"

"You obviously got wind of this whole KINGPIN shit." "Yeah I herd the shot god".

"Well nigga?"

"Well nigga what? People calling you The KINGPIN? That shit don't bother the god none if that's what you're wondering. I told you long time ago this shit and this day was coming. Told you the day would come when someone would have to step out front and be, for whatever reason, accountable for this shit that we got. I also told you that I like fucking these bitches and slappin' these bitchass niggas too much to be out front. It takes a certain nigga for that shit. Now if you can't be there I got you, but for the day to day operation of this shit your the right man. As long as you and I know the truth and the money don't stop coming, I don't give a fuck who the head is perceived as being. We've really got to scheme even harder now."

44

"Yea I know."

"Once this thing has a so-called head, that's what the competition is going to be aiming for. Not only that, it will be obvious that this is not just some kids from the city bullshitting with a little dough. Many more groups will recognize us as being much more."

Yo, what made you do that shit to that runner in front of that kid and all? Why didn't you just kill the kid?"

"Ra, I was thinking about that but I feel that the kid may be our link to some of these new heads out here who don't realize what you and I and this crew have gone through and accomplished out here. Not to mention some of the fresh ideas may be for the better."

"Whatever. I knew you took a liking to this kid and I know why regardless of the shit you are saying".

"What do you mean by that?"

"Nigga you know and so do I".

"Look, have you noticed that overall production has been up on almost all levels."

"Yeah, I've noticed but I don't credit it to that bitch-ass kid."

"No I mean it seems like everybody is taking care of B.I. more seriously."

"Everybody except them ho's. Why don't you cut them bitches loose and we can start some gambling spots, pool halls or even some telemarketing shit. Anything but them stinking, arguing bitches. And then there's that Pam. Man listen, we don't need that bitch! I can keep my foot in them dancers asses."

"See that's just what the fuck I mean Ra. You would want to go upside their heads every time they were a dollar short. That ain't always the answer."

"O.K. GOLDIE, I mean THE MACK, I mean Superfly the pimp. You got it all figured out but I'm telling you as long as the money flows fuck them hoe's, they could all gobble my dick!"

"See that's another thing no damn Finesse. Sometimes it don't always call for a slap or a pimp stick. Some kindness and understanding in the game can get great results too. Plus you would be wanting to fuck the bitches all the time. And that shit is definitely a no-no."

"Man fuck that, if them bitches is working for us they can fuck us."

"Na see that's were the respect comes in."

"Whatever ICE T."

"Look, in a way I do credit some of the shit that is going on to the kid. Because he has stepped up his production, very subtly all the others have started to do the same. I say we do a big push and see just who the fuck is serious about this shit. I say we push everybody till they just about bust so we can get enough money to do this Tele-vacation scam thing the right way. The shit hit me like a thunderbolt. Ra I can see us in a two hundred thousand dollar a month business if we push it right."

"That's my nigga. What do we have to do to get the numbers up to and past that point."

"Well I ain't got all of the angles worked just yet but if we put our heads together and stay low key and patient, I think we can really be seeing some real serious money by the summer."

"God, you talking about staying low-fucking-key and motherfuckers all over Brooklyn is fucking calling you KINGPIN! How fucking low key is that?"

"I think we might be able to use that to our advantage. But it's gonna mean that we will half to groom that kid and fast. You'll half to stop steppin' all over this kids chest."

"Man fuck that little bitch he'll do right or I'll dig a hole for his ass."

"See there you go. It ain't gonna work like that. We need to let some of these motherfuckers see that their hard work is paying off. We also need to let them handle some of the shit that we're spending our time doing. And we need to go and do other more important things. I was reading in this management skills book that in big companies they call it 'delegation of responsibilities'. And you, my man, are gonna half to start wearing some more elegant gear, not Timberland's and leather all the time."

"Wait you got this fucking master plan out of one of them dumb ass books you be checkin' for?"

"No. Not the plan, just the part that frees up our time so we can keep getting paid. Man just trust me, we're really about to hit the big time with this shit!"

Next Level of Doing Things
("The Meeting")

I knew it was time for some major shit to happen. All the city was watching and at the time that was most of my motherfucking world. I had taken a few days to get out of town and get my shit together. I was convinced that I was going to run the city, at least my part of it. I could not come back guessing, I had to be sure of my shit. Even in front of Ra, my trusted compadre from many years back. I also realized that I'd made a mistake by sharing with him that I had learned something from a book.

Ra, though, wasn't as ignorant as he was acting. His ass stayed up on everything from torture tactics used by the Filipinos to the goddamn e-trade. I think there were parts of him that didn't want me to know that he was smart. Or how smart. I had made my mind up that C.C. was going to play a bigger part in what the fuck was going on. I had worked at little bullshit jobs in the past. I noticed that they never tapped into the ideas or talents of half their employees; even when they had good ideas and shit. That wasn't going to be me. Keep in mind I also realized we wouldn't exactly be having anybody's fortune five-hundred board room meetings either.

I came to see how this whole KINGPIN thing was a lot for a nigga to live up to. Mainly because everybody had a different thought about what a KINGPIN was. You basically had to be all of that shit to those different people. When I'd go out on one of my mysterious sabbaticals, no one really knew where I was. I'm sure they thought I was in Cancun or some old Jay-Z music video shit, but that was only what I did on vacations with the crew. On solo missions would be more along the lines of deep Virginia, to some property my Grandfather owned. This was a house that was old but had all the modern conveniences, if you wanted them. I would use the fucking out-house that my grandfather had built with his own hands. I also chopped my own wood for fires and cooked all of my own food. I needed those experiences to keep me humble and understand that prison would be much harder than this if I was to get caught slipping.

There was a female that I could fuck who had no fucking idea who the hell I was. She lived down there. Though I used to ruff it, certain shit I just ain't going without. The broad's name was Billie and she was a cool ass chick. What I liked about her was that she knew how to just lounge. I met her at the grocery store down there. She was one of those people who never left the town they were born in. Billie never asked any questions about who I was or why I was there she just liked to chill with me. I never asked her about why she didn't have a man I just knew that she did not have one. She did have that spunk about her that I liked. I think if she had been born in the city and had been exposed to more, she probably would have either been in the game or working for a big firm or something.

After satisfying my country jones, I came back to the city with a vengeance which I intended to pass onto the whole crew. For starters, I had very private but informal meetings with the people I felt were going to be key in the next few steps. I had changed the plan from trying to make the name of this crew respectable enough to do business with other crews to making the name of this crew so respected, revered and feared that others would try to put us down with their shit to legitimize them! Some of these "meetings" for lower-level members were held at nickel-plated shotgun point.

C.C. and I would have to have quite a talk. She was going to have to show her loyalty in other ways other than just getting the job done. She was going to have to start following orders to the letter. No more slick renegade shit. I slid up to her place and I asked her to take off all of her clothes. She headed without hesitation.

"Any idea why I asked you to do this shit?"

"No," she said, "but I'm glad you did. Briscoe I have always liked you. I just hadn't got around to fucking you. Plus I wasn't sure how you were going to act about the shit. You know you nigga: so damn private. Everything with you and that asshole Ra is such a fucking secret."

"Is that right? Tell me more."

She said she liked the fact that I was all about my money. C.C. also said she liked the fact I didn't fuck the hoe's I had on payroll and didn't let my crew do it. I asked her to close her eyes and keep them closed.

"That's kinky," she giggled, "but cool we can do kinky!"

I asked her to lay back on her back, which she did. I then told her to spread her legs open as far as she could and pull her ankles back to her ears.

"I knew all that stretching from Kung Fu was gonna come in handy!"

"Keep your eyes closed and don't say a word while I strap this motherfucking condom on."

"I always had a feeling you was packing some real shit but my legs is wide as shit!"

"You gonna like this steel I'm bout to give your ass."

"That's what the fuck I'm talking about".

"Don't say another word." I had put a condom around my nickel-plated forty-caliber Taurus pistol. I slid the barrel right up in her shit. I mean up to the trigger. "Okay, now open your eyes and don't say a motherfucking word and don't put your legs down neither." I told her how shit would be from now on and reminded her who the fuck was running this shit.

"Now what you got to say about that?" I asked when I was done.

"Damn that felt good motherfucker. It's been a week or two since I had a good multiple! Oh, about that shit you talking about, I am completely with it. I have been waiting for you to give the go ahead and I think everybody else will fall right in line. But look now that we got that straight what about some of that real steel? I feel one more multiple coming on."

My pager went off and it was business. "Sorry, gotta go get this money."

"Well, you know your way back here."

As I bounced, she yelled out the window.

"It was good but you owe me nigga. I like your style but I still a want some of that sweet meat, KINGPIN!"

Who Got The Props?

I was so glad to get the hell out of her spot. I didn't know what to do. Don't get me wrong at some point I always knew that C.C. and I might fuck, but I damn sure didn't want it to be that day. Plus, I needed C.C. to help in the grooming of Young Bleed. There are things that a man cannot impart to another man. Even though Bleed was young he was still a man. My next step was to go and have a little talk with him. I was not sure who was best suited for the assistance in the grooming of Young Bleed.

If he acted like he had some sense C.C. might fuck him on a humble. That would be the worst thing in the world for him. He doesn't need the feeling of power to be overwhelming for him. I'm sure C.C. was going to do what she said and tell everybody that she had done a little something with me. If she in fact did that then went ahead and fucked Bleed he'd be thinking he was fucking with the same bitch KINGPIN fooled with. That'd be too much power for a young lieutenant to have.

On the other hand, if I turned Bleed over to Ra for exclusive tutoring and he acted a fool or didn't follow instructions to the letter or if anything out of place occurred, Ra would kill him on the spot. No second thought. Ra would then say some shit like: "the kid got on my nerves and had to go, so I threw him away, fuck that kid anyhow." Don't get me wrong, Ra provided a good example for certain things, but it was best if I was present when the teaching took place.

I eventually figured it would have to take a little of each of them, and a lot of me. I pulled up to the kids rest and went in. I had keys to all of the apartments and there were no chains on the doors only a gang of fucking locks. I caught the kid in bed with some young floozy bitch. I pulled steel on his ass and sat in a chair. I waited about twenty minutes before his ass woke up. He was startled.

"Don't move", I told him. "Now wake that stinking bitch up and tell her to get our breakfast going." The kid was slender in build but not skinny. He had put on quite a bit of muscle since he'd been down with the crew. "You won't always have a pistol," I once told him, and after that he started going to the boxing gym and bulking up a bit. One thing that I did like about the kid was that once he found out I wasn't about no-bullshit, for the most part the motherfucker listened to me.

"What's up with the early wake up and shit? I thought I wasn't supposed to meet you until 11:30."

"Yeah, well, the time got upgraded…and so did you."

"What do you mean? I've been doing everything you told me."

"Did you hear what the fuck I said?" I glared at the kid as he rewound the tape in his head.

"Oh shit, I got promoted! That means I got wild juice now!"

"Relax motherfucker. Calm the fuck down and listen to what I'm about to tell your ass. This ain't no joke or no boys club. This is a very intensely run criminal organization. One which your ass really ain't got no business being down with this early in life. The shit is far advanced from the average bunch of clowns who hold down a few blocks in Brooklyn. The difference is we got some niggas with a whole lot of knowledge and good sense running this shit. Not to mention, a gang of fucking experience, and most of all patience. What's happening is that the whole organization is making wild power moves. You are in the right place at just the right time but your ass could fuck it all up with one wrong step. This is only a trial position for you. I don't like the word 'acting' in front of a position. That's for those corporate motherfuckers. But put it like this: One fuck up and your ass is not just demoted back to your old position, your ass is out. And by now you know there's only one way out. Here's the deal, you will be in training. You'll be very close to me, and close to Ra as well. So you better piss them problems that you got with Ra out. Bottom line, Ra is your motherfucking boss, superior and whatever other title he happens to come up with. You'll do what the fuck he says without hesitation. You won't be calling him sir or no shit like that but be not mislead: if he wants you dead, your ass will be as dead as Caesar. He and I will never separate. You will always have to answer to that guy, so if you can't get over it you might as well say so right now. And God forbid anything ever happen to him. I've got other cats that I'm close as shit with that you'll never see until the time comes. So disregard all thoughts that if Ra weren't around you'd be *the one*, because you still would not be in the top spot. In the streets you will be shown great respect, fear, envy, sometimes-large amounts of hate and occasionally some doses of love. This organization privately does a lot for community and that's one of the reasons very few of our crew spends their time going back and forth to jail. At the same time there's a gang of people getting paid the hell off. You're only being told these things because you need to grasp the seriousness of this shit."

"So does C.C. know about all this shit?" he asked.

"C.C. knows more than you, she also knows what you know and won't tell you nothing you don't already know. But by no means does she know everything. The only ones who really know the full scoop are Me and Ra. And that's how it's gonna stay." I asked Bleed to tell me about this floozy-ass bitch that was making breakfast.

"Oh, that's Sheila. I've known her for years, she's cool as a fan."

"Is that right," I replied, eyes circling the room. "You sure do have a lot of trash bags in this joint. When do you ever take them down to the incinerator."

"I was gonna help Sheila take them down this morning before my untimely wake up call!"

"Come on kid, we'll take them down together. But look, first I've got to tell you that you will have to prove that you are in this shit for life. You'll have to bump off an enemy of ours so you can make your bones."

"Fine, no problem. Just tell me the who and the when and where."

"So you don't have a problem killing for the crew or anything?"

"Nope; anything for Fam."

"I'll let you know the who and what nigga it will be and all of that shit at a later date. For now, let's get this rubbish outta here."

Bleed hollered at Sheila on the way out. "Yo baby breakfast ready?"

"It will be in a few minutes." Bleed asked her if we had time to take the trash down to the incinerator first. "Yeah, there's time. Let me help y'all"

I then whispered to Bleed. "Damn, good looking out. That chick of yours is cool." We were up on the ninth floor so we all hit the elevator together. We got downstairs which, as usual, smelled funky as a pot of old chitterlings and greens. Plus the boiler was going so it was both noisy as shit and hot. We still had to go down more stairs and down the hall, where half the lights in that bitch were either dim or gone all together.

"Damn nigga, it's time to upgrade. This apartment is cool but you got to go through all this shit just to take the fucking trash out. I see why it was piled up."

As we got to the incinerator I could see someone standing there, it was Ra.

"What the hell are you doing here?" asked Bleed, surprised.

"He's supposed to be here," I answered, before dropping my trash bag and pulling out my heat.

"What the hell is going on?" cried Bleed.

"Told you that to be in this there'd be a lot of sacrifices you'd have to make to get in, and even more sacrifices to stay in. Didn't I warn you you'd have to make your bones by killing somebody?"

"Yeah, and didn't I say no problem. Just waiting for you to point the nigga out and he's dead!"

"No Bleed, don't think you understand that would be too easy. I need you to go ahead and take out this broad."

"Who?" cried the kid.

"You know who," returned Ra.

"Naw man, not Sheila, she's been like my girl and shit for years. She's always looked out for me and all, I got love for her."

"Yeah I know Bleed, that's why it's got to be her. I told you your only undying loyalty must be to this."

"Brisco, I mean Kingpin, please anybody else, anything else but not her."

"Sorry Ace, this is what it takes to run Brooklyn and that's what you said you wanted to be part of." He took an unsteady step back and said, "I won't do it."

"That's a shame," said Ra. "Guess I'll have to fuck this cute bitch in her pretty pink butt hole before I kill her ass then. Because believe you-me, this bitch ain't leaving this motherfucking room; you can bet on that."

"That's a fucked up thing to do to me man. I told you I love her".

Through all this, the chick never said a word, almost as if her ass just didn't believe what the fuck was going on.

"So what you love her," continued Ra. "Just get it over with. It stinks down here and it's fucking hot."

"Come on Ace," I added, "just hit her in the jaw, knock her out and strangle the broad so we can throw her in the incinerator and leave. Either that, or let Ra do his job. Then join her. You wanted those *props*, right?"

Hard as it was, the kid performed the task. He again had one tear running down his face but he somehow sensed that what was happening was necessary. He also knew that he would die with her in that room if he did not commit to the instructions.

On a certain level, this was the reason for the partying every night and all the pretty girls. The good times kept us too busy to concentrate on the pain and havoc we had reaped throughout our lives. I gave the kid a hug around the neck and told him though I knew it hurt, this is what it took to live the way we live.

"You two ready to go now?" Ra asked. "The bitch is in the incinerator and I want a 40. Plus that bitch's underarms was musty anyway."

Rest assured, the decision for Bleed to kill the girl was not a hard one. It took little thought. It did take me back to a time when I had done despicable things in the name of allegiance to the cause. I gave him the extension of the hug because at this point, Bleed was like steel being tempered for a future function.

If done too quickly, it could warp. If done too slowly, its density could make it useless for certain purposes. But if done with a strong and patient hand, it would pass the test of time and endure the elements. In this case the elements to endure would be the management of one's own emotions. Mostly, the balance of guilt of deed and profit of greed.

What To Do With Pam?

Having promoted Bleed and having the talk with Ra and C.C., it was now time to figure out what to do with Pam. If Pam and the semi-brothel were going to continue to be one of our enterprises, it would have to be stepped up considerably. Ten to thirty grand a month would have to be brought to a weekly dividend. Otherwise it really would not be worth keeping. But what was coming in was still too much to give away. I didn't feel that expansion was the answer for this.

It would, for the most part, just bring in more of the same and it's cost might not be justified. Ra's take was to "put the bitches that we already have on some higher dollar clientele."

"Now how do you suppose we do that?" was my reply.

"First we stop fucking with that club! Let's open our own club just for that shit and keep everything. The bar, the door, the pool table money part of their tips, I mean everything!"

"Now that's the motherfucking Ra I know! How come you never dropped this on me before?"

"There was no need but this is the new order of the day, so I'm with it."

I pulled Bleed aside to let him know that's exactly what I mean about Ra's mind. You never know when he's gonna go gangster or genius on your ass, but when he does the shit works well. All this time I had forgotten that Pam was a bartender back in the day. I had Pam come and meet with C.C., Ra, Bleed and myself. Pam being Pam, first thing out of her mouth was, "my girls got their money together so I don't want to hear shit about no fucking money Ra. And C.C. you know how I feel about your ass!"

"And bitch you know how I feel about your stank-ho'in ass," C.C. shot back.

"Well bitch your mama pussy stank cause your daddy had a dirty dick beeeach!"

"Wait a minute," I said, "you motherfucking hoe's can stop all that catty bullshit right motherfucking now. Cause I ain't about to hear it. Look, I hate to say it but Ra is right. I did not call this meeting so that you two could fight it out. One of the reasons that I did call this meeting was so you could understand what's going on. This whole operation is about to start making some very major moves. The one thing we will most certainly need is harmony among us. Now I'm not talking about you two shaking hands like little kids in the fifth grade and still beefing every time no one's looking. I need some real motherfucking harmony. Now can I get that?"

For the moment, neither chick was willing to budge.

"Oh, nobody wants to say anything. Let me rephrase it. This crew will have harmony or the un-harmonious members will be out. And you all know there's only one way out. So I'll ask the question again, Pam and C.C. do you have harmony?"

"Yes we do" They both stated.

"God damn right you do. Your asses better be close as the Pointer Sisters in this joint. Now that we've cleared that up, there is a building that is vacant two doors away from Master's Barber and Beauty Salon. C.C. this is our salon that you currently manage and run. If it's possible, we'll be taking that building and turning it into a very high class 'Gentleman's Lounge'. This is where we'll be able to turn some very high tricks. I'm talking two and three hundred dollars a pop and about fifteen girls on duty around the clock. The cover for the place is that it is members only and mostly a place for executive pool players and top level businessmen. This has got to be a place where the big money comes to play. In order to have that, the girls must be top flight as well as the other services. Pam, you will still basically run the place but you will do so from behind the bar. This way you can see who comes and goes. The upstairs of the place will be off limits to all employees. I mean all. This is a place were only the top cream spenders will come. Ra, I need you to talk to that Alderman that stays in debt to us all the time. I think he may be able to pull a few strings for us when it comes to the Department of Liquor licenses. I want this place to be completely legit."

Accidental or not, Ra suddenly busted out into laughter.

"See that's the shit I'm talking about. If we're really about to compete at the level we're talking about, we will have to have some legitimate businesses that make real income. I mean taxes and all. This will allow us to do even more illegal shit. Pam I will need you and the rest of the girls to take two months off so we can get you together."

"What do you mean get it together? My shit is together."

"No, I mean really together. We'll be sponsoring your asses to the ladies gym. Them hoe's will all be doing aerobics and weight training as well as reading some fucking books. If them bitches can't get themselves enough discipline to read at least the fucking newspaper, we don't need them. The type of people that you will be servicing will not tolerate no ignorant-ass bitches. Nor will they put up with shit coming up missing and all that petty shit. I mean it goddamn it! I want all of them to get their masseuse licenses. A lot of the bitches we have will not make the grade, but fuck'em. We're taking everything to a higher level. This means cleaning a few dead weight type motherfuckers out. Not only that, but I don't want none of them cussing around the clients."

"Clients?" asked Pam. "Since when did a bunch of trick-ass niggas and/or crackers become clients?"

"Since we decided that long money is better than short money we need at least a minimum of fifty grand a week to walk out of this place. That's just for starters. To bring in that type of dough I will need the proper bait. Which in this case is some classy-ass bitches and a classy-ass atmosphere. Ra, any suggestions?"

"Yea, if we gonna have this place pop'in like that we're gonna need some type of security in it, and I don't mean ADT."

"You're right."

"Not only that, why would you have a place like this in the district that we're talking about? It seems that this shit should be in Manhattan or something."

"I feel you. But what I've noticed about crackers is that they will put whatever they want in the heart of the ghetto and won't give a fuck about the crime or anything. So I'll use the same tactic. Not only that, this spot is supposed to be a getaway for these clowns. Some place where their wives' private eyes and investigators won't go, and won't follow. This is just that place."

"I don't like it," said CC. "The idea is good but I don't like the location. Ra is right. There is a lot going on over by that shop."

"Yes, but not enough to keep you from making money! Look, I don't think you all have any idea how much clout this crew has amassed. Those same little bitch-ass niggas you think are going to be a problem, work for you! They are trying to sell the shit that they bought from us, or from one of our constituents. We can re-route where they sell their shit, or cut the supply off so they have nothing to sell anyway. That's what the fuck I mean by juice!"

Bleed jumped up out of his seat. "Goddamn, how far does this shit run?"

"Further than your mind can understand," returned Ra. "Now finish with what you were saying B".

"Look, if you go to Washington D.C., the RFK Stadium is in fucking N.E. The area is full of crime yet they still have the Budweiser Superfest there every summer. Chicago has a multi-million dollar sports arena and it is on the fucking ho stroll. So why is it that we can't have an executive men's club in Brooklyn? If you think about it, this is just what the fuck we have been waiting for but the shit is gonna take work. Pam your ass is gonna be a very important part of all of this shit. Did you keep your bartender's license?"

"Yes I still have it, and it's still current, I'm a little rusty but I'm sure the shit will come right back to me."

"Good. That's the type of good sign that I'm talking about."

"Look Kingpin, two of the girls already have their licenses".

"Good look'in Pam."

"Look, I don't particularly want this shit right next door to my fucking salon. I've been working there a long time and I don't need a bunch of horny crackers going back and forth, fucking with my flow," complained C.C.

"For starters bitch that shop is not yours. Ra and I own the deed on that shit. Second, it'll only help you to be down with this new move. If you can show me where this is going to truly make your shit non–functional, I'm willing to listen. Otherwise, shut the fuck up! The only thing that really matters at this point is stacking more money and clout. If the Menz Club makes more than the beauty salon than the problems this presents don't matter. I will not close the salon but this is going to happen and you all need to get used to that shit. Furthermore I think a few of you might be getting this mixed-up with a stockholders meeting or some shit. This is a meeting for the people we would like to see survive with this crew. After being down so long and having been good loyal members, I felt it was good to hear what you thought. But in no means does this mean anything has changed. This is still some shit that Ra and myself started and will always run with or without your asses. Is that shit understood?"

"Yo, I just think that she meant…"

"Shut the fuck up Bleed! I don't need no fucking interpreter. I know what the fuck she meant. This shit did not grow out the ground like a tomato. This was done on purpose. Those of you all who can't follow instructions to the letter and perfectly to the tee, might as well take a shotgun to your heads right now because that will be the result from this point on. It's got to be that way. Look, with the amount of money we've been generating also comes a certain amount of heat. Which means that along with the new amount will come new heat and new pressures. It's our job to out-smart these motherfuckers and try to keep every thing running. We can't do that if we've got to be worried about all the little details, which means we've got to be able to trust you guys to run shit to the letter. Not kinda like it was told to you or something like what you are supposed to do, but exactly what you were assigned to do. And you should be relaying this same message to your underlings. The new penalty for even the smallest infraction is DEATH. Pam you got something to say?"

"Yeah, that's a lot of pressure on my girls."

"No Pam it's a lot of pressure on your ass because I don't have time to deal with every whore who fucks up a few dollars. But I will take time out of my ever-so busy schedule to come and kill you. I told y'all that we were taking this thing to the next level and

I wasn't bullshitting. We are running this shit like a NFL or NBA team. We all know that the coaches are always the first to go. Not the people in the owners box, which in this case happens to be us. And definitely not the draft pick player which is the folks who work under you. I need not say our slogan again: *'There's only one way out'*. In fact, I want you motherfuckers to all say it with me goddamnit in unison."

"There's only one way out."

"Now that's more like it. Are you in or out cause I don't need you I'll let the welfare feed you! Pam what's the verdict?"

"I'm in, but you sure are pushing this thing to the limits."

"You're damn right. We're gonna get the same amount of time if we get caught so we might as well ball-till-we-fall. Anybody got anything else to say. The room was silent.

"Let's go get it all," declared Ra.

I knew for a fact that shit was gonna be a little tricky for a minute, so I made sure that me, Ra and Bleed went out to the clubs a few nights in a row. See that's the one thing that always seemed to make everything all right. Bleed was still getting over the woman that he had just killed. But if he was living his dream he wouldn't have much time for all that mourning shit. All I could do was make sure the kid had the best time he could because the next few steps the kid would take would be dangerous as a

71

motherfucker. I really didn't want to see the kid dead, but there was one hell of a chance that his ass was not going to make it from week to week. This was a lifestyle that many wanted but few actually had the balls to go after because you usually die long before you get anywhere near the top.

How I had been so successful at such a young age was like the eighth wonder of the world. For this kid to come along and try to duplicate that type of success was more than unprecedented. It was for the most part impossible. I was having a growing concern for Ra's silence. I didn't want him feeling that me taking the reins so to speak meant by any means that he was not as useful because, for real, that was not the case. I would be needing him now more than ever before. In the past, he'd always been happy with the title or at least the unwritten title of enforcer.

But like all things, after you get them and enjoy them you can stop appreciating them. Or sometimes you can simply outgrow them. For this to work I would have to use all the tools I could find. Keeping in mind, that I still had to be many different things to all these different people.

For the most part I had done a pretty good job of being penny smart. Now it's time to see if we were going to be pound foolish or not.

Best Kept Secret

The last few major group discussions were basically the confirmation of things everybody already knew. The stakes had been raised considerably, all across the board. As far as the security in The Menz Club went, I was still a little shaky on that. What I had wasn't quite what I wanted but I had someone in mind. I thought my man Tino would be good, but I also knew his tendency to get just a little too wild at times. So I had other ideas.

"Yo what's up B?"

"Yo! What's up Leek? What's the runnings?"

"You know same ol' shit".

"I feel you. How you been doing?"

"Well to tell the truth not so good."

"What's up? I told you if you ever wanted to get back down I've always got a spot for you. You're the one who is always saying that you don't want in anymore." Kaaliq had gotten into some beef early on and didn't want any trouble anymore. Well, what really happened was between the ages of 12 and 16 his ass got caught a few too many times. He had a real rough time dealing with prison life. Hell, if you're a kid jail is jail. You don't have anything to compare it to so to you the shit is hell. Plus Leek's people were blue-collar workers so they didn't have much, but we didn't have anything. So for real Leek didn't need to do what we were doing. Plus I don't think in his ass he really wanted it like me and Ra did. In the early days he did pull his weight and he was pretty good at the shit. He just had a small bit of bad luck and got caught. Once he was inside he couldn't really handle the shit and the sharks moved right in. He wasn't a bitch or anything but he had a lot of fights and shit with some of the older guys and I think it really affected him. He told me that he'd made a promise to God that he would never get mixed up in the game again (unless he had no other choice) if only God would let him get out unchanged. Two weeks later on a technicality his case got overturned. He attributed it to God answering his prayer and was never really involved in the game again. I always offered him work and shit. He always said it was appealing but he was doing fine. The fact was for quite a while he had not been doing fine and the toll was starting to show. When he came to me and said, "What's up B?" I sensed what was up.

"Finally, you came around?" I said, happy as shit! To me nothing could be better than having my closest friends get paid right along with me. Especially when they were as smart as Kaaliq.

"Wait a minute," Leek said, "I don't really want back in. I'm just tired of barely making it. Plus, it's time for me and Angie to get financially ready for the next few steps in life." Angie, of course, was his lady. They had been together for years. I guess by that he must have meant kids or something. I really didn't care about the reason, I was just glad that he was back in.

"Look it may be better if only you and Ra know I'm down. Or how far we go back".

"Fuck that, I'm throwing a party and all that shit. What are you talking about just me and Ra knowing?"

"Listen, everybody knows that y'all got the hot hand and are making all the right moves. But there is always a few in the bunch who ain't with it. By me being on the outer fringes I could kinda be your eyes and ears along with whatever else you got me into. Not just listening in the fam, but also on the concrete."

"See Leek, that's why I miss your ass. It's the little ideas and shit you be hitting me with."

Ra and Leek always got along great so I was sure there wouldn't be any problems. Kaaliq was an avid pool player so I figured he could sort of be the HouseMan for the Menz Club. This would give Pam the help she needed and take care of security. I proposed he handle day to day operations with Pam.

In case of a problem, final word would be Leek's. Then of course it would come to Ra and myself. I asked him if he could live with $1500 a week.

"Sure B," he said. "I knew you would play it classy."

Doing Wrong

Over the next six months things would go exceedingly well. I was doing everything right, or so I thought, until Ra pulled me up and told me I was fucking up spending too much time with this one broad. Naturally, I went in defense mode.

"What the fuck are you talking about Ra? I'm on the block and in the office! How you figure I'm giving too much minutes to one broad?"

"Look, you remember when we used to watch them old gangster movies and shit, and we used to say how it was always greed or broads that took the tough guys out?"

"Yeah, I remember."

"Well you and I have gotten this far because neither of those two have affected us. I know you will never get too greedy or anything, so what does that leave?"

"Broad's! You think I would let a bunch of funky-ass broad's get in the way of what the fuck we've been working a lifetime on? Hell no! You know better than that!"

"Yeah B, I know better then you letting a bunch of broads get in the way, but I'm not completely sure about this particular one."

"Just because I've been going out with the same woman a few times don't mean that a nigga's getting soft."

"Look, this ain't Young Bleed you're talking to. I've known your ass too long for you to bullshit me. Listen to you, 'I've been going out with the same woman'. Since when did a bitch start getting called anything but a bitch? You've been on the scene but not on the scene for a minute now. I'm just telling you that this ain't no time to have your head up your ass. The shit that we've been working for is really starting to happen for us in a big way. Don't let this bitch fuck shit up for us."

"Wait a minute. This lady is just a nice woman that a nigga's been checking on, this don't mean I'm about to get married or no shit. You're acting like I asked you to stand up for me or something."

"Look I spoke on just what the fuck needed to be said. Now you handle it any way that you see fit. But put this to work in your mind, you aren't the only one who has worked hard to make this shit happen. And you're not the only one who stands a lot to loose."

78

"Listen to me Ra, we've been living the life as far as a bunch of girls go for years. We've both been in the bed with two or three broads at the same time and all that shit. I just happened to meet a chick whose cool and acts like she's got some sense. Why would you want to skunk this good thing for me by pissing on the shit?"

"I ain't pissing on shit, but let me ask you this: What kind of example are you setting for your little protégé bleed? He was forced to make sacrifices but now you want to play lovey-dovey with this freak. Enough said nigga, I'm out. I've got to go and check on the MENZ Club. I don't want you to be late for your uptown date."

"Damn!" I thought to myself, mad as shit, as Ra broke out.

I wasn't sure if I was mad as shit at him or me. I'd indeed been spending a good amount of time with Nicky. But it was so uncommon to find someone who had the qualities that she had. She was fine as shit of course. But that wasn't the thing that really sold me on her. It was the fact that this broad never asked me any dumb-ass questions about my lifestyle. Most women always had a lot to say about the hours I kept. Or they wanted to know why I always came by their cribs so late at night. Some even pestered me about why we ventured so far out the area whenever we did go out. But Nicky never quizzed about any of that. She was always glad to see a nigga. She didn't care if we were fucking or going out to diner. She was just glad to have me around.

I'd met her in the elevator of my lawyer's office. She worked in the building and I'd peeped her in passing down in the food court. But I never said anything because I was always there for business. It just so happened that on this particular day our eyes met and next thing you know I'd asked her if she was hungry. She replied that she was actually on her way to lunch at the moment. I asked her if I could join her and she said no problem. After that we just started hanging out every now and then. But a part of me felt if Ra had noticed a difference in things maybe I was hanging with Nicky more than I should have been. Ra seldom said anything to me about business. So when he spoke, I took him seriously. It would be a sacrifice but I would have to cut her back considerably if my dealings with her affected the company.

Could it be that Ra wanted to stay forever youthful, content at playing the playboy gangster with these ho's? Or was it that I was really getting tired of the unsteady assortment of women in my life? Either way, if the shit was affecting the business it had to be put under control.

As I drove late that night a lot of things started running through my mind. I must have drove all over New York that night. I drove past all the old clubs we used to frequent. The Puzzle, the Rooftop, The Palladium, Latin Quarters, The Fever, The Roxxy, The "Q" club. The Soap Box was where I saw the

Sugar Hill Gang get down, live! There was also The Garage and The Tunnel. And who, of course, could forget Bentley's. My mind wandered towards all those old spots where Rakim, Kool G Rap and KRS used to get down. I'd watched the pendulum swing from Shante to Salt and Pepa; from Lil Kim to Eve. From Nice and Smooth to MOBB Deep and more recently from Biggie to Bow Wow. Was I sick of being one of 'them niggas that's gettin it' or was it just that I buggin off of this uptown freak? Fuck that, thought. This is what we wanted to be. On top of the streets and we'd just about achieved that shit. I couldn't allow some classy uptown shorty to fuck up all we've worked for. Plus, like Ra said, I've got Young Bleed in grooming, watching my every move. I quickly grabbed my nuts and got my head together.

I came to the conclusion that Ra was right. I had gotten just a little off focus and it was his job to pull my coat on that shit. Thing now was that I had to make sure nobody else had seen the same shit that Ra had peeped. I was due to meet with Kaaliq in about twenty minutes, so I figured I'd better get a move on.

No sooner than I arrived, I saw Pam in the club.

"How the fuck have you been?"

"Cool," I said.

"You sure about that?"

"What the fuck you talking about Pam?"

"Your boy Kaaliq is a trip."

"The fuck you mean by that?"

"You have a minute?"

I glanced at my watch. "Yeah, but make it quick." Pam then told one of the girls to watch the bar, as I led her away.

"Step up into my office."

"I would rather talk to you in the stock room."

"Fine," I said.

"I know that this nigga is your man from way back. Not because anybody told me straight out but because this nigga is fucking a lot of the girls in between his pool games and watching the place."

"WHAT?"

"Look don't get huffy with me nigga! I'm telling you that your man is acting like a fucking trick! I'm not saying that he's fucking a bitch now and then. This nigga is doing two and three bitches a day. And some times two girls at once. You said that with the new way we was doing shit we need to police each other. Well, I'm telling you that with the time he's fucking them girls they need to be with paying 'fucking' customers. Not gaming with a nigga that should be watching the door and my back while I'm serving up this liquor. Now don't get me wrong, the nigga is sexy as shit so I know why the girls like his ass, but that's not the reason that his ass is here. And you know that I'm not on no snitch action but you also know that you said that this is how it should be. We supposed to be keeping each other sharp! Plus the nigga has a little bit too much to say to them girls.

He's told them all that he's your man and that y'all go way back and shit. He also thinks his ass is running this club. Now that's not what you and I talked about. I told you I'm not working for this nigga. I don't give a fuck who his ass is or used to be cool with. Far as I'm concerned he's just a new ass nigga to me!"

"Wait, wait, wait, you've told me enough. I'm not trying to hear who's losing at the crap tables. Damn! But look, I'll take care of the shit and keep your name out of it. So just relax."

"Relax? Fuck that nigga I'll shoot his ass if he steps to me with any of that dumb shit! I was doing you and Ra a favor because we go back. But that new-ass nigga could kiss my ass and you can tell him I'll give him five minutes to get a crowd together."

"Ah Pam shut the fuck up! You did the right thing don't fuck that up by running your motherfucking mouth so much. Damn! That's why you aren't further along now. You always got to talk so much shit."

"Yea and I'm gonna keep on talking shit!"

"Now Pam, I'm gonna say this one more time and I don't want to hear you say shit afterwards. You did the right thing and I said that I appreciate the shit. If you can't leave it at that…."

"I get it. But damn your ass sure is edgy lately." I shook my head and strolled off to find Leek.

"Yo Leek I need to see you in my office for a few ticks."

"Sure thing God what's up?"

"Let's wait until we get in the office to speak."

"That's cool."

"Do me a favor, close the door and pull up a chair."

"Listen to you 'pull up a chair'! Sound like Bogart or some shit."

"Look Leek, I don't think you're getting a good understanding of what's going on here. This ain't a bunch of kids playing crime boss in Brooklyn. This is for real!"

"Yo, what are you talking about B?"

"What's this shit that I'm hearing about you playing grab-ass with the girls and shit?"

"Ah come on man. So, I had a little fun with a few shorties. What's the harm?"

"The harm is that those shorties are bringing in $1500 to $2000 dollars a day. They can't make any money sitting on your face. Unless you about to start paying them!"

"Oh it's like that now?"

"Look, you walked away from this and said that you wanted nothing to do with the game. I'm not gonna sit here and throw the shit up in your face but I will remind you that many of the people around you have been in the trenches and they don't get half of the privileges that you get. So I'm just telling you not to take the shit for granted. Not to mention the fact that you're supposed to make a certain revenue at them tables. You can't do it on top of some broad."

"Yo, you know what? I noticed that the other cats don't really get at the girls that much. What's up with that? Them hoe's is fine as shit!"

"The fact of the matter is that the guys who can come and fuck with these chicks have enough pussy from real butter broads out in town. You're really playing yourself by even being seen with these freaks. You got Angie at the crib and I know you still got a good mouthpiece. Why would you want these pro's when you could get you a regular broad that's cool enough to be your regular bitch on the side?"

"What, like that uptown broad you got blow'in your whistle? Yeah man, I told you I'd be your eyes and ears. You thought nobody knew about the bitch! But I've heard about the bitch."

"So what? A nigga gets some pussy uptown and niggas act like the fucking sky is falling!"

"Alright, you care about the bitch. Cool. But you gotta play it like you don't. Some of these bitches around here treat you like you're their man. What's that make them feel like when they see you spending time and money on this next bitch?"

"Hey look, they work for me. I don't answer to these ho's. Plus they have seen me and Ra at the club with bitches before."

"Yea that was you and Ra and that was a few hoe's, not you chillin alone in Benihana's, eating at candle light with this bitch like your ass was Mr. Roaurk on some fantasy island shit."

"Fine already, you've made your point."

"Have I made mine? Yeah, I'm supposed to hit you guys off with $3,500 a week and y'all are hitting me with $1,500. How does that make sense?"

"Look man this is an organization. It takes a lot to keep this shit a float. Do you want to know what we charge outsiders just to come in this joint and play? Look, Bleed could use your help on a few collections tomorrow. I want you to go and help him. Take a few days off from the tables."

"Yo B, I said I didn't want to get in too heavy."

"Look if you're in you're in. If not, let me know what time to tell Angie you'll be home for diner. This is how the shit is being run. I'm glad you're back down but you're still gonna have to pay some dues. Otherwise I can give you some lookout work which pays about 50 bucks a day, out on the crack strip. I don't think you have the proper grasp of how large this shit has gotten and what kind of work had to be put in to make it this way. I feel that a little time in the field would do you some good."

"So wait I'm taking orders from you now!"

"Look, you and I will always be friends, but yes at the present nigga you are taking direction from Ra and me. You don't have to take orders from anybody. You can always break back to the pots and pans you were washing at the hospital."

"How'd you know about that?"

"Yeah nigga, I got my ear to the cement too."

"I got to admit, what motherfuckers say about your ass is true, but it always has been."

"And what new rumor might that be?"

"Your ass is The Kingpin nigga. You don't miss a step, except with that bitch," chuckled Ra as he left my office.

I knew if this many people had noticed the fact that Nicky was important to me that it was time for me to chill for a few. About three weeks went by and I didn't really think about anything else but business. This was what was needed. Ra was right, I'd been a little delinquent in my watching out over Young Bleed. After I put Leek with Bleed for a few days he was back to his old self again, thoroughly on-point like the Leek of old. I had thought he was going soft for a second there. But after he got his knuckles a little bloody he turned out to be just fine.

Bleed on the other hand was doing well with business but was partying just a little too much. The power over the little ghetto bunnies was maybe too much for him. I wasn't sure if it was that or the fact that he missed his old girl. Usually in the life we lead, we almost never mentioned the dead, especially if it was someone we had bumped off. But this was an exception. I caught Bleed fucking some stupid bitch in the fucking bathroom of the Menz Club. This was not one of the girls who worked there. This was a girl he'd brought to the club. I waited in the bathroom until he was done.

"WHAT THE FUCK DO YOU THINK THIS IS?" I asked, surprising the shit out of him. "You gotta do your thing, go get a hotel. Or come ask me about using one of the rooms upstairs. You don't fuck some bitch in the bathroom of this club."

Out of nowhere Ra walks the fuck in and immediately slaps the shit outta Bleed. He was damn near unconscious but the wall was keeping him on his feet. He looked for a split second like he wanted to do something about it, but when our eyes met he knew that it was best for him to take the hit and call it a mother-fucking day. I think the kid always looked forward to the day when he would eclipse my loyalty to Ra. I didn't agree with Ra doing the shit in front of the hoe, but fuck it. The shit had happened now and I wasn't gonna say shit to the contrary. Before I could say another word Ra was in rare form.

"Bitch ass numm-nutt nigga. What the fuck you think this is? Your mother's house? You get your small balls and this come guzzling bitch the fuck outta here."

"Yo, PIN I didn't mean to…"

"Shut the fuck up don't nobody want to hear your moaning and wining. Just get the fuck out Bleed."

"Yeah BOSS."

"My office pronto! And loose the bitch."

I took Ra to the side for a private moment.

"Yo Ra, you sure were hard on that kid."

"Look what the fuck is going on here role reversal? You put this young-ass kid on cruise control then want to step foul to me for staying in his shit!"

"Na, I wasn't stepping at all. I was just saying the kid is getting a little age on him. You don't have to embarrass the kid at every turn."

"Look I wouldn't care if that piece of shit was thirty. He knows better than to pull off a stunt like that in here. This ain't no playground for his ass. What if one of those lawyer's, had come in and seen that shit? What do you think that would do for business?"

"You were absolutely right Ra. The kid was definitely outta line. I agree with what you did in every way. I was just saying that the broad did not have to see one of ours like that. But fuck it, you're right, I have been slacking so I don't really have the right to say too much. I'm gonna talk to this kid in my office though."

Bleed came into the office on some apologetic shit but I wasn't trying to hear his ass for real.

"Look your ass has been getting a lot of pussy and having a lot of fun and I'm glad for you. This is all part of the game, but don't loose sight of what we're doing. This shit is no joke. If you let your ego get the best of you your ass could easily end up dead or in the can forever."

"I know but you wouldn't let that shit happen to any of us. The word on the street is that our shit is unstoppable and you and Ra are possibly the best to do it since Bumpy Johnson in the twenties. He didn't die all fucked up. They say that he died an old man with all of his grandkids around him and shit. That's how I'm gonna go out."

"Ace that's not guaranteed. You never know how shit could go. Lots of crews have come and gone from the scene. And lots of them are sitting in jail or dead! Don't get it twisted. Just because we are up today don't mean it will always be that way. Guy Fisher got all day fucking with this shit. And he bought the Apollo."

"I talked to Swanson and he said that in all the years he's seen niggas come and go, none have been as big as you and Ra. At least none have been as smart".

"You patterning yourself after Bumpy is cool, but remember that Bumpy went to jail and took a lot of losses in this shit. All I'm telling you is that you had better stay sharp and fucking concentrate. What about Sheila?"

"Yo, fuck that bitch. As far as I'm concerned she is a casualty of war!"

"Oh you on some real tough guy shit now."

"No it's not that, I'm just saying that she was the price of me getting to where I wanted to be".

"Is this all that you wanted it to be?"

"No, I want more! Even though I'm getting more I want to get it all! This street shit ain't shit compared to what's really goin on. When you gonna put me on some of the in-door action? I'm ready."

"I told you I'd tell you when you're ready. Your ass ain't going no where if you keep on doing stupid shit like fucking some bitch in the bathroom of the Menz Club. Now go call C.C. and tell her to meet me at the salon in two hours."

"How should I know her number? She don't even talk to me on those terms."

"Go and get the number from Pam and call her. You want more juice, well start getting more shit done. You need to learn as many people's jobs around you as possible."

Two hours later C.C. met me at the shop. I asked her how she was doing and you can believe she told me.

"Look, I am busting my ass and I want more clout".

"What are you talking about?"

"For starters I think I want to go full time with this shit."

"C.C. look, you have your own shop you are making damn good money why would you want to fuck all of that up or take a chance with it?"

"I want that bitch Pam working for me and I want to get more money. I'm watching you and Ra get a lot of loot. I don't mean a few hundred thousand, I mean everybody knows you two are really getting it! You think I'm gonna continue to participate in this and not get paid! I think you could take John Bronson and them down if you wanted to. That would really make you cats legends in the game."

"I hear you," I said, before slightly shifting gears. "I want to know once and for all what is really going on between you and Pam? What is the real beef?"

"Well you know any time you have some women involved in some shit there will be some natural catty-ness going on. Plus I want some of that sweet meat your ass got and I have a funny feeling that you have fucked that bitch. I want all those inches nigga, and I'm not gonna let you continue to put me on this street level backburner."

"Yo, you have plenty of male friends C. This would only create problems down the line."

"Brisco you know that I've always fucked with you. I look out for you in all situations as it is. Why not let this just be another activity we share?"

"Yo hold fast, it's my celly," I said, reaching for my pocket. "Sorry, but I've got to bounce. We'll finish this another time. Until we speak again, I will give what you said about going full time some thought. In the mean time, keep an eye on Young Bleed, the kid's coming up fast, maybe too fast."

The Step Out

"Yo, Ra it's good to see your ass."

"Yea nigga, seems like lately we never get to just kick it anymore."

"Look, I was thinking about us getting away for a minute."

"What do you mean a minute?"

"You know just be out for about a week or so, like we used to."

"Yeah nigga, that does sound good."

"Just step out from this shit for a few".

"Where did you have in mind?"

"I don't know but it can't be too far cause we might have to get back quick."

"What about Philly?"

"Cool, that's just like being here."

"Let me guess, we're gonna chill with that nigga Joey Crillz right?"

"Yeah, what's wrong with that?

"Nothing I guess."

"What, now you don't like Joe?"

"Nah, it's not that I don't like the nigga, it's just all that pastel shit he be wearing. What's up with the plaid shirts and Gucci shoes and shit? To me the nigga is a bit of a soft touch."

He ain't no punk but I ain't into all of that fashion shit."

"Look, he's from Philly. You know them niggas is on some different cute shit anyway. Plus nigga you didn't like the suit shit until you started seeing how much ass it brought about. But you can't deny that the kid be handling his BI."

"No doubt. He's got that town locked down pretty tight. There are a few cats around, but he is consistently the number one nigga there. He just don't seem the type to put in the work."

"Maybe he has a thousand loud simple motherfuckers on payroll to handle that part of it. Either way you shake it, the kid gets the work done."

"Alright then, Philly sounds good. I need to check on my man Tino anyway. I wanted to talk to you and get your thoughts on bringing Tino in for a little work."

"Tino is cool, he's my man too. Thing is, when you and that guy get together…"

"Don't say it, bodies show up all over the place," chuckled Ra.

"We don't need that shit right now. I need you to tell me that you will keep a handle on a lot of all that wild shit."

"You got it GOD. Word is bond you got it."

I swear Ra almost busted out into laughter. I knew this shit would make him happy. What I was doing was getting every thing in place. I knew this shit wasn't gonna last forever and with the greed level I was getting from everybody on a private level, I could see these niggas was heading for one hell of a fall.

We got to Philly and Joey Crillz was there, glad to see us niggas, well at least glad to see me. He liked Ra but said that the nigga did a lot of unnecessary shit, and I couldn't call Joe a liar. But Ra was my man. Joe did wear a lot of shit that I wouldn't wear but that shit had nothing to do with us being friends. He had to find some way to get bitches to suck his dick, and however he pulled it off, I wasn't mad. I was more the bottom line type. Did the guy get the job done? Not how, or what he had on. Did he get it done? Plus I thought the stuff that he put together looked cool on him. Anyway we were in Philly and all was well. Joe had some choice ho's on deck. The club spots were a little different, but that's sort of what we wanted.

It had been three days and nobody had heard from Tino yet. I knew this nigga was up to some old show-off shit. While leaving the mall, here comes Tino in a drop-top Bentley. Not the new joints, but one that was about ten years old. This nigga had the system BLASTING ridiculously, with three fine ass bitches on fucking motorcycles giving some kind of ghetto police escort. This nigga had two more broads behind him on horseback, while he's sitting up on the trunk with a white mink coat on like he's the Mayor in a parade. This cat looked like he'd lost his goddamn mind. But that's ghetto love. You had to love him for even thinking to pull off some shit like that on Broad Street, in November no less. I knew at that moment that this was gonna be a lot of fun if we didn't end up in jail.

"Yo B, what you know about this shit?!" barked Joe.

"C'mon now, you know this ain't my style," I shot back.

Funny thing was Joe almost didn't want to be seen with this cat. I could understand, it was his territory and he did have a rep to protect. Tino had a rep too. But his rep was as pretty much a hired gun. He did some collecting and extortion but for the most part he was a self-contained unit. I knew that he always wanted to be down with us but Ra had never mentioned it to me. If he did I would basically have to O.K. the shit. But Ra also knew that Tino didn't take orders very well. If he was down with us he would have to take orders. And take them well. I think that's the reason that Ra never mentioned it. Tino and Ra had a real strong relationship. They had sent each other dough at times and Tino sent some money to Ra's fam when he was biding once. This wasn't anything that I had not done as well. But I did recognize the bond. We all embraced the wild nigga and the good times began. We had top-flight broads. I mean TOP choice shorty's. Joe had taken all the proper precautions. I mean the whole time we were there we had the best that Philly had to offer in whatever we were doing. Keep in mind we all had dough, so it really had to be some real bonkers shit to impress us. I ain't gonna front, I was open. Joe and I took a stroll and he looked at me carefully.

"How much longer we gonna live this?" he asked. That shocked me a bit.

"Where's this coming from Joe?"

"I can see it and feel it. We've gone about as far as we can go. The powers that be ain't gonna tolerate us doing much more than what we're doing. And neither one of us really wants it bad enough to make the sacrifices it's gonna take to control shit on the next level."

"Joe what are you talking about? We got this shit by the tail."

"Yeah right, you know better than that. You done read too many of the same books I have to still be living that childish dream about controlling this shit until you're old and gray. You know what happens to us in the end. It's only one of a few things. I know that this little trip is more than just a chance for y'all to come and spend dough in Philly too."

"You think you got it all figured out."

"No, cause if I did I wouldn't be having this talk with you now. I have always admired some of the smart moves you've made. But lately some of what has been coming to me has not made much sense. It don't seem like you. I know your game is sharp. And I don't see it slipping no time soon, but we have done all that there is for us to do. I'm starting to feel old in this shit and you got in this shit long before I did. And I know for a fact that you've got a few years on me. So if it's wearing on me you've got to be feeling some of this shit. I mean, what are you gonna do? Buy the Brooklyn Bridge and shit? What am I gonna do? The Liberty Bell ain't for sale."

Then it hit me. This cat is setting up for a quick out. "You know these niggas ain't gonna make it without you Joe."

"To be honest, I don't see my crew lasting too far without me either."

"Check it out Joe, if you look at the so-called 'greats' that came before us, they made some mistakes that we didn't. They also went out in a kind of fucked up way. All of them except

Bumpy, he just bounced one day and that was that. I was thinking about doing something like that. But I feel responsible for what happens to these cats."

"Look, these people are all grown or at least grown in the game. Let's just bounce."

"That shit is easier said than done. I also feel sort-of responsible for you. Who are you taking with you? What about your moms, your sister all your fam? They won't be able to make this trip."

"Shit! You're right B, I never thought about that shit."

"You had better. Let's put this on the back burner for now and just know that it is on the table."

The trip continued and we never said another word to each other about it. But I knew it was on Joe's mind. I could see the concern in his face every now and then. He had always been close to his moms and sister. Just the thought of leaving them was going to take some getting used too. I myself was close with his mom. She used to cook for us and let us crash at her house. She was always cool. I didn't have the same concerns about leaving that Joe did because I had long ago decided that this was what I wanted. My family was either in the wind somewhere or dead. My family for the most part was the members of this organization. Mainly the top players, Ra was my twin brother. Leek was my first cousin. Pam was, well I don't know what the fuck Pam was. C.C. either. But for sure, Ace was that wild younger brother that

100

you had to keep an eye on for his own good. And of course Joey Cracks was my man, always.

Amazingly enough Tino and Ra were on good behavior. They just chilled with the girls and ate and drank a lot. Which was what we were there for. I was surprised but I also knew these cats were not going to keep the wild stuff down for long. Tino, Ra and myself had a talk concerning him coming in. I told him that if his ass had any problems being an Indian he might as well stay right where he is. But he saw things differently.

"Look, you and I both know this has been on my mind for a while now. I like you B and I like the way that you do shit. I also know about my rep, but a lot of that has changed. I'm getting older and I can see the benefits of being with a group instead of always being on some solo action."

"Yeah Tino, I can sure tell you've changed," I said with a hint of sarcasm. "That stunt you pulled on Broad St. had all the signs of a changed man. It'll take more than you chilling for a few days to prove that the old loose cannon Tino Bailey I know is dead."

"I didn't say he was dead, I said that I've changed. The action on Broad was just to celebrate my homies being in town. Is it a crime if I miss chill'in with you fellas?"

I turned to Ra. "Ra you haven't said much. What spot would you see Tino filling?"

"Well I think some of the figures have been a little down on the dope strips. He could work those, do a little enforcing and collection work. That would free Bleed and a few others for a move up."

"Oh now that's rich Ra, I mean really rich. You want me to believe that you want Tino to handle the dope strips to free Bleed up for some inside work? Since when did you start thinking that Bleed was due a promotion?"

"Well the kid has been putting in a lot of work and this would be good for everybody."

"Putting in a lot of work? It wasn't that long ago that you were slap'in the shit out of this kid for fucking some bitch in the Menz Club."

"Well that was just *grooming* the kid you know *seasoning* him to the ins and out's and out's and ins of the game. You didn't hear me say that he had not been doing good work though."

"Okay I see where this is going, Tino. Get the fuck out for a few ticks." Surprisingly, without hesitation he grabbed the doorknob and bounced. I looked at Ra. He knew that I pretty much had to go along with this shit. Just like he had to go along with Bleed.

"Sure you okay with this Ra?"

"I think it'll be better than you suspect."

"You think so. Let's see how ready Tino is to take orders. Not only from you and I, but from C.C. and Pam. I'm gonna go along

102

with this, but I do feel a little funny about it. Just like you did with Ace. I'm saying that you need to be prepared to take care of his fuck-ups if they arise."

"Cool God, I can live with that".

"Now where on the rank structure do you want Tino to fall?"

"Let's put him at lieutenant status. That puts him right were Leek is. I feel that's reasonable."

On the way back in the limo we got a page saying that Ace and two of the runners that work under him were in central booking. I knew the fun couldn't last for long.

Them Damn Dogs

I was in the limo when my pager and then my celly went off. It was Pam talking about how Bleed was at central Booking.

"What do you mean Pam?"

"You heard me, him and some other clowns are in central booking."

"For what though?"

"I don't know," she shot back, "but one of my sources said that they were in lockdown for some shit that had something to do with them dogs bleed be keeping."

"Alright, do me a favor. Have C.C. call my hotline right now."

"I'll do it, but why don't you think I can handle the shit!"

"Look Pam, I don't have time for this shit, have C.C. call me now!"

Two ticks later I had C.C. on the phone.

"That was fast," I said. "Were you standing right next to Pam or just on the other line?"

"What the fuck are you talking about? I haven't talked to her since last week. Anyway, I called to let you know that Bleed and two of those morons that he keeps with him are at Central Booking."

"If you didn't talk to Pam how did you find out about it?"

"I got a man on the inside down there that I used to fuck who keeps me up on who gets popped for what and when. But look, I called your lawyer, Mr. Agronsky. He said he'll have their asses out and at your control room and he'll keep them there until you or Ra come get them. So what is this control room he's talking about?"

"Yo C.C., you handled that perfect. I'm on the outskirts of the city right now, I'll see you later tonight or maybe tomorrow morning. This little deed just may have bumped you up to full-time status."

"But B, what the hell is this control...?"

CLICK. I hung the phone up on purpose, because some things she didn't need to know.

Ra was all over the place. He wanted to know what the hell was happening and rightfully so. I told him what little I knew and we agreed to leave Tino with Leek for a few ticks until we got the situation under control. Of course, Tino was more than willing to try and prove himself. But the situation didn't call for that as yet.

We took Tino over to Leek and Angie's. He was having his dinner and shit. I brought him up to speed and asked him to take care of Tino, which included taking him to the Menz Club and updating him on the basics of how things were done. I warned Leek to keep the intricate details to himself for now. But the truth was he himself only knew the fringes of the business. I did that so that Leek would not feel like this new face was coming in as his equal. I always felt you had to think ahead of these cats and sometimes think for them.

Ra and I both knew we had a long few days ahead of us. First we had to trek all the way up to Jamestown, New York. This shit is fucking past Buffalo. We had a guy who had a bad gambling problem and made a deal with us that we would collect the rent on his apartment building for the next four years. This worked great because we didn't want to own the thing, it was a dump. But the basement had six apartments that we used as a lab for cooking coke and cutting dope. The place was great for that but we had long since found better uses for the property. The other apartments were filled with our other employees. These were cats that had drawn too much heat for one reason or another and needed a place to chill. The apartments that were not being used for laboratory services had been transformed into what Ra called the 'Control Room'. To me it was a metal medieval torture chamber. As of yet, no one we'd taken there had ever returned.

Mr. Agronsky had been my legal mouthpiece for many years. I was locked down with his son once where some kids I knew from the neighborhood were gonna rape his ass until I intervened and got a dude I knew to give his son a pass. Strictly based on my friendship with the dude. The dude sorta owed me for helping him cheat through summer school one year. I knew the dude would honor my favor request if I could get to him in time. Turns out the dude's boy already had the head of his penis in this Agronsky kids' ass. It was really gonna get bad for this kid. Needless to say, I saved the kid in the nick of time, and he and his father never forgot it. I had no idea what I was doing at the time, but it turned out I'd just received an 'in' with one of the best criminal defense lawyers in New York. I think he let his son go to jail to teach him a lesson, but he had no idea where they were sending him.

Anyway, Agronsky knew what was what and over the years he grew to really like me. He never cared for my dealings with Ra but he didn't interfere. Agronsky was not completely clear of vice himself. He had visited the Menz Club with a few of his clients from time to time. I asked Mr. A if he could stay until we got there?

"No problem Brisco, but I'll have to leave shortly after that because I've got a flight to catch and I must be in court in the morning."

We got there a few hours later and I asked Agronsky what the outcome of this was gonna be.

"Look, I'm not sure," he said. "I think I can get them off but the real heat may come from the guy's father."

"No problem. His father will have to live with it or go away."

"No I don't think so," he responded.

"What do you mean?" I asked.

"This guy's father is a Senator. I know you have a lot of power but I don't think your trying to fuck with a member of the United States Senate"

"I know that's right! What are the charges?"

"Willful endangerment. Loosing a dangerous animal. You know the usual foolishness."

"Damn Mr. A, you can't beat that small shit!"

"Yes, but keep in mind that the original charges were attempted murder and the sort. I've already got the prosecutor to give me the pictures of the bites."

"This was a serious attack. The public is already about to ban those dogs anyway. So it's probably not the time for a big stink. If that's not enough, the clown had a crowd of people who saw the whole thing."

"Wait, they've got witnesses?"

"No, when the cops showed no body saw anything but you know how that goes."

"Look 'A', so what actually happened?"

"According to the one story I got, the guy owed money for some crack or something and your little Three-Musket-dumb-asses tried to make an example of the guy in front of the whole projects."

"Bottom line, can you clean this up?"

"Yes. From the legal stand point I can. But this guy's son is gonna need damn near a new arm and you'll have to cough up the money to smooth this out-- under the table."

"What are we talking?"

"I'd say three hundred grand ought to clean up the mess. But if the father gets a hard on for the shit we could see real problems from this. If it was me I would let this kid swing in the wind and disassociate myself from him. Or let him show up in somebody's river. If you catch my drift. Now I know that's your little man but if they tie this kid to your organization it could be problematic!"

"Shit! Ra what do you think?"

"I think we should let Tino escort them down to Florida and let them take their chances with the gators. Let's talk to them first before we decide anything."

"I'm gone guys, got a plane to catch. I'll stay in touch. It will take a month or so before this shit comes to court if it goes that far."

"Look 'A', before you go witch one of them actually set the dogs loose."

"Report says it was Mark Morris and Jason Tammiz," Agronsky informed us.

"That's all? What about Austintine Havolice?"

"Oh he was just there. Cops said they thought he was with them but it wasn't clear. He actually only got charged with loitering and disturbing the peace. I thought M and M was your little man. That other kid was really just there. He doesn't have to show up for court. I got his stuff dropped by the magistrate, though he doesn't know it." With that, Agronsky took off.

"Ra what do you think about that shit?"

"It just may have saved the life of this piece of dog shit but those other two clowns are as dead as Abe Lincoln."

"No doubt! Do you know how you want them to go?"

No, but I can tell you it's gonna be painful."

"No shit let's have a go at it."

We enter the control room and Ra has these cats spread wide, chained to the wall like slaves.

"Which one of you stupid motherfuckers did it?" I ask. "Tell me which one of you just cost this group all this fucking money!"

'M & M' was first to speak. "We were just setting an example that people can't be late paying us, that's all."

"Well how much money did the clown owe *us*."

"Two-hundred dollars."

"That's all? You're telling me that over a small time debt like that you started all these problems? I can't even get the buttons on this ostrich coat fixed for that little amount."

"And what the fuck do you mean by owed 'us'?" demanded Ra. "That's our money. You two pieces of garbage, you taking liberty with our juice?"

"No, I just mean that..."

"Shut - the Fuck - Up! This is what's going to take place. One of you is going to die a gruesome horrible death. The other will return to the ghetto fucked up in a wheel chair and addicted to heroin. We'll see to that! The reason for your return is so that you can be an example! Round piece of dog shit!"

Ra starts in with the hammer, I've got the softball bat and I'm going to work on knees and hips. Not two minuets into it M&M cries, "what about Ace?"

"I thought you would never ask," said Ra. "He didn't turn the dogs loose on that Senators kid. But we've got something special for his ass."

"Look Ra, we didn't know that the kid's pops was a Senator," pleaded Jason, as I shifted my attention to Bleed.

"Bleed, you will stand there and watch what happens to these two clowns. See, you're responsible for them because you were the ranking official. You won't die but you've been bumped down a notch."

"And that's worse, cause I know your little simple-ass wants to run shit," added Ra. "But you don't know how. The reason B is the front man is because I didn't and don't want to make the sacrifices needed for that position. You can't imagine the shit you've got to go through. All you see is the fucking glory. That's one of the reasons that I never really liked your ass. If that lawyer hadn't said that you weren't involved directly, I'd be whipping your ass right now."

I then turned to the other two, sizing them up.

"M&M, looks like you're the winner, you will get to go home. Snug as a bug in a rug. A full carpet that is. I don't want your funk offending the neighbors. You will be found in a week or so, after the rats in your apartment pick your dumb-ass down to the nub. No one will hear you yelling because your mouth will be tapped with enough duct tape to hold you till Christ comes back. Hope you don't have a cold. Because your last breaths will be taken through your nose. 'Set an example' my ass. You idiots were trying to start a little name for yourselves. Well now you have one. You are those two dead asses that set the dog loose on that kid. And suffered behind it. Now as for you Jason, may I call you jay?"

"Come on man don't do this. Please, I'm not the one to go out like this. I don't deserve this shit. We made a mistake man. Ain't you ever did something you regret?"

"Yeah, letting you two clowns get down with an organization like this. But like Jay Z says 'you gotta learn to live with regret', and I can live with this. How about you Ra?"

"Live with what? These two, shit I feel worse after eating too much pizza!"

"Well, Jay where were we? First-off, Bleed un-cuff his right hand. Jason I want you to grab your testicles."

"Man please whatever you got n mind don't do it. Wait!"

"Ra did you hear that?"

"No, what?"

"I hear the bitchings of a little girl. I thought it was a mouse. But upon further investigation I find that it's Jason. Bitching! Now Jason I want you to follow my instructions to the letter. That's the reason that you're here. You don't follow instructions very well. But we're gonna fix that, ain't we Ra?"

"You know it."

"Again –Jason, grab your nuts. Feel good, don't they? I want you to close your eyes and remember that feeling. Because you will spend the rest of your life in a wheel chair and you'll never feel your dick or nuts again. But what you will be able to do is tell everybody you fucked with our money and this is your outcome. Ra would you do the honors?"

"Of course god. But you forgot to tell him about his new friend. The one that will always be there for him and never leave him alone."

"Know what Ra, you're right. Thank you for reminding me."

"Yo Ace tell them we didn't mean any harm," Jason screams.

"Ah, Young Bleed did you have something to add?" I ask. "Please, speak the fuck up, don't hold back. If you have some advice or words of wisdom, share them with Ra. So I can have him skin you like a cat in a Chinese restaurant! Fuck that Ra, I've changed my mind, I'm gonna handle this myself. Jason I'm gonna hit you in the small of your back with this softball-bat continually until your back breaks. Or this bat breaks. I'll know when you can't feel anything because when I'm done I'll poke your feet with this nail. When they don't respond I'll know it's time to order your wheelchair. You'll stay up here for about a month and get your heroin addiction going good; then we'll release your ass to the city to fend for yourself or fiend for yourself. Then you can begin setting that example. Ra you got M&M right?"

"Told you god, he's dead as Abe Lincoln."

"Then it's done. Bleed, get the nail," I ordered.

The screaming was horrid. I myself thought that maybe we'd gone too far. But when I thought about the three-hundred grand that these fools had cost me, it seemed more like justice. Surprisingly Bleed got the nail and played his part well. He was just glad it wasn't him, I guess. I stayed upstate for a few days but I kept in contact with Leek, Pam and C.C.

Killing that kid was too easy. I should have felt more remorse but fuck that, he had made an expensive fuck-up.

I received a call from Ra telling me that M & M was dead. He was found in his apartment by his cousin around ten o'clock. When he was found he was well decomposed and funky. Ra and I spoke in a code that would not allow recordings to decipher what we were really saying. Five Percenter's often did this. Ra was due to escort Jay back to the city any day now. I decided it would only take a few powerful doses to get Jay where we wanted him: to be the perfect hopeless dope fiend.

Meanwhile, Bleed and I still had to address what exactly would be done with him. He had tried to speak to me about it twice and I knew that his ass was concerned.

I decided after a good meal and a cigar to ask him what the devil he was doing with those two clowns.

"I was assigned to those two," he said.

I asked him if he was aware how close to death he'd come.

"I didn't know it until you broke out the bat and the hammer that Ra had."

I let him know I still had love for his ass but if the case had called for it, he'd be dead. After explaining to him that I just happened to talk to Mr. A on his way out the door. He understood just how close he'd come to seeing Christ. He asked me what he could have done differently. I told him that leadership is something that life teaches you. There is no exact handbook. If there was, everybody would be buying it. One thing is that those two greedy clowns were not the ones that he needed not to keep an eye on. I also knew that he had a real affection for dogs. And this sounded like his handy work. I said that the moment a crowd appeared he should have brought everything to a halt. Plus, I cautioned, you have got to know who the hell is buying product from you. Especially, if they're a new face.

"But PIN this guy owed us, I mean you-all, dough. What about that?"

"The amount wasn't enough to credit what you did. I have people in line for that little shit. He has been buying from you and will continue to buy from you. Turning those dogs loose will cost twenty times more than two hundred. If you don't want to end up like that clown M&M, you'd better keep your shit right. This is the last time I'll be reminding you."

When Ra got back I told him that I had straightened the kid out. But the demotion was still in effect. I don't think Ra cared one way or the other. He was still celebrating that his man Tino was down. I asked Ra if he wanted me to take care of Jason or what?

"Nah, me and Tino got it."

"But Tino is all the way back in Brooklyn."

"Nope, he's out in the car," said Ra, which surprised me.

"Oh you really think that he's ready to be privy to information like the control room's location?"

"He don't know where the fuck he is. I just thought I needed to bring him up to speed on a few things and the long car ride was a good place for that."

"Look, you take care of Jason and I'll take Bleed back to the city. I think we need to really be visible with all these bodies and foolishness going on."

"You're right, we should get back on the scene. Who knows what the fuck Pam, C.C. and that bunch have been up to?"

"I'll meet you at your place in a few days B."

"Cool," I said. "Now look, I know Tino is trying to be your shadow and shit but don't bring that cat to my rest. And don't forget, just like Leek and the rest of them he too must turn a profit."

Back to New York

We'd been back to New York for about two weeks and things were going okay. I got a call from Agronsky, telling me to come to his office. I dash over and he tells me things are fine on the legal side.

"What happened to those young guys was for the best."

"What do you mean?" I ask.

"Well with them both dead there is no one to prosecute."

"So this cannot possibly affect my industry?"

"Correct," he tells me, to my relief.

While I was happy with A's news, I wasn't sure about what he meant by them both being dead. I didn't put too much on it at the time, but it hadn't got past me. It so happened that my lunch date with Nicky was front and center on my mind. I'd kept in contact with her almost every other day. She was excited about seeing me. I can't front, I was looking forward to seeing her as well. It'd been a minute since we really spent any substantial time together. When I studied her face, I could tell she had other things on her mind besides her enthusiasm with seeing me.

We went over to her place, where I discovered she'd heard about that dumb-ass M&M on the news. Somehow she knew the organization had something to do with the shit. She asked me if that's the way it had to go down. Of course I played like I didn't know what the fuck she was talking about. She went for it in a half-ass kind of way. I flipped the subject, informing her that I wanted run some real serious shit by her.

"What's this all about baby?"

"You know that I've always had my own company, right?"

"Yes, I know," she said.

"Well I've been thinking about, maybe, switching gears a little."

"What'd you have in mind?" she asked.

"Well, was thinking about taking a year or two to go to school or something."

"That sounds like a good idea. It's obvious you've put a lot of time and thought into what you're considering. So how long have you been thinking about school?"

"Been thinking about it for a while now."

"Well I must say I am impressed," she declared.

"If I do this, I'll probably go to school abroad. What are your thoughts about that?

"Are you asking me to go with you or do you just want my opinion?"

"Of course I'd love it if you could go with me, but what about your job?" I inquired.

"I've told you before I can do what I do all over the world. But let's look at this first, you still did not ask me to go. I'm not one of the people who work for you. If you want me to go you will half to ask me and have a more finished plan. I wouldn't just be going as your playmate."

"Oh, see, there you go with the phony."

"Look, I love you and I'm glad you have a new ambition but I also want you to respect the fact that you're asking me to leave everything I have here. Not that I mind doing it for you, but I want you to understand that it's not easy and I wouldn't be even considering this if I did not love you. I'm not some little girl from the ghetto who's impressed with the cars and jewelry. I'm a woman who's impressed with the man and his potential."

"Okay, you made your point. I value that fact that you're so ready to roll. But right now it's just in the planning stages. I have a lot of loose ends to figure."

"Have you made plans for your friend Ra?"

"No! -- I mean not as of yet. Not sure if he's ready to go into something else yet. Look, what you've said has made a lot of sense. I think I need to be alone for a while. You mind if I tip off a little early?"

"No it's not a problem, I fully understand. But I want you to know, I love you and whatever you decide I'll walk through fire with you if that's what it takes."

I missed my Menz Club and I wanted to see it again. It seemed like a long time since I'd just sat in the chair in my office. I can't describe the feeling. The place was nice but I had been in many other places that were better. There was something about the fact that this was headquarters for the empire I'd built with Ra. Amazingly enough, things were pretty much the way I'd left them. Pam C.C. and Leek had done a wonderful job. The orders all the way down to the booze was correct. But there was still something that didn't sit straight in my mind regarding Agronsky's comment: "with both of the suspects dead." He said the case was closed, but didn't know what he really meant by that. So I gave him a ring.

When I inquired about it, he told me they'd found the beaten tortured body of one Jason Tammiz in the park. I finished the phone call like nothing was wrong. I paged Ra right as I got off the phone. He hit me back and I asked him if he was near the club. He said he was right down the block. Cool, I thought, before asking Ra to stop past when he had a chance. Ten minutes later he was there. I asked him what happened to Jason.

"That little piece of shit is dead, he had the nerve to try and spit on Tino."

"But Ra I thought we agreed this kid was not going to die."

"Yeah but this clown tried to spit on Tino! So you know how that go."

You O.K.'d it for Tino to kill this kid? Or did he go out old Tino style?

"No, I gave the thumbs up. We didn't need a witness running around anyway."

"Know what Ra, you're right. We didn't need that. But you and I usually discuss shit like this. Plus you didn't speak on it before."

"Well to tell the truth I was enjoying it too much."

"Enjoying what?" I asked.

"You were the "Brisco" of old for a minute there. You actually seemed to enjoy the work again."

"Yeah, but that was only because those clowns had messed our money up. And what do you mean the Brisco of old?"

"You know, ever since this 'Kingpin' shit your ass has been a little different. You take all this shit serious as a ma-fucker. I mean every detail."

122

"Man attention to detail is what keeps niggas like us on the street and not in somebody's box, or jail. But tell me this Ra, why'd the lawyer have to tell me that this clown had meet his end?"

"Man look B, the kid was in route to the hood and he started with all this 'fuck you niggas, I wanna get high shit.' I told him to shut the fuck up – he spit on Tino. Now he's dead, and that's it."

"Alright, that's the end of it. Check it out, I also wanted to see what you thought about bringing C.C. in full time?"

"I think it's cool god. Is that what she wants?"

"Yeah, she said something about it before we left. I think she handled the situation really well with contacting Agronsky and all."

"I agree god, she did do a good job with that shit."

"I was also thinking of taking a little break with everybody and introducing Tino formally and all."

"Sounds good to me, where'd you want to do all this?"

"Was thinking about maybe The Palladium?"

"Yeah, sounds cool. But wait ain't the Palladium closed?"

"True, but I say we open it up for a night. We take the dough we make from that one night to cover the expenses incurred from the group trip."

"Damn god! You really breaking out all the stops for this one."

"Well, look, other than this last little mishap we have a real tight crew. I think it's time we let 'em blow off a little steam. You wit it Ra?"

"I feel you!"

Party's Over

The party was a big success. No problems at all. The crew was surprised when I told them we had a mandatory meeting right after. They were even more surprised when I passed out tickets for everyone to attend the carnival in Trinidad. They all had a real good time, especially C.C. Since she'd been promoted to full time status and she was excited about it. Pam didn't seem to care one way or the other which really caught me off guard. I thought there would be a little beef or at least something said. But there was nothing.

The return trip gave all of them a chance to get their focus back on the game. I still sensed that I was on my last leg of this shit. Ra and Tino had been spending a lot of time together. I wasn't jealous or anything. I always knew they both liked a lot of the wild side of the game. I, though, was mentally preparing my out, though I still wasn't sure just how I wanted to fade. I was thinking more and more about some of the things that Nicky and I discussed. She'd made some good points but I was not completely sure that I wanted her to skip with me. Living on the move was not for everybody. To me she wanted some kind of ironclad blueprint, but this life didn't always go like that. Plus dating in the city is different from really being about a person all the way. I had let her come to the party but not as my escort. She came instead with one of her girls. Nicky blended in, but I could still tell she was out of her normal element. At the same time, she later told me she was surprised how many people were there that she thought she'd never see in that environment. My nigga Joey Cracks came through and brought some of his crew from Steak Town. This was a good thing for me. The kid always kinda added that little touch of class to things. He wasn't able to make it to Carnival. I was disappointed because he was from Trinidad and I thought he would have made my stay a little better. All in all things were fine. I remember thinking I'd better take a few ticks to speak with Pam and C.C.

Separate discussions would be best.

A Talk At The Waldorf

I spoke with C.C. first.

I figured having her meet me in my suite at the Waldorf would work. It was quiet there and I knew we wouldn't be interrupted. I scheduled her for a massage in the lower section of the hotel. I made sure she had a little bubbly in her. Only a glass or two though, which was nothing for that girl to guzzle down. Looking back, all this may have been a mistake. I was trying to get her to relax and think clearly. At the same time I wanted her to celebrate her little promotion, and to understand what it meant. I told her she'd have a lot of responsibility put on her and that the same penalty which fell on others would fall on her.

"I'll do anything for you," she said, expressing her total commitment.

I told her how I noticed she often told me she was doing things for 'me'. I asked her if this was something that 'she' wanted or not. If she was only doing it for me, she should stop today. C.C. went on about how she'd always liked me as more than just her employer.

"Look C.C., we been through this before."

"No we haven't," she replied. "Before we were talking about just the sex. I'm talking about you and me."

I felt myself growing impatient. "Look, you'd better get all this stuff about you and me out your mind. You and I have made some money together and I don't see why we can't continue to. You have this thing in you head about you and me being on some Bonnie and Clyde tip, but that's not it! You'd better except the reality of your situation! You work for me and Ra. Anything else is speculation. You will have to make your money drops and do everything that any other person would have to do. That includes murder! Not mutilating some nigga that you're fucking, for a gag. I mean real, cold, murder! If you can't stomach the task, you'd might as well say so right now.

She looked at me kinda funny and said, "first off, why are yaul still trippin off that nigga's little scrotum problem? That's all niggas want to talk about, 'C.C. cut off some niggas dick!' Shit, that white chick Bobbitt did it and don't nobody think nothing of it. I cut a useless body part off of a clown and the shit is all over New York! Furthermore, I resent the fact that you look at that as just some gag. I thought it was some of my best work. And it *was* over money. Future money. I needed to do that so niggas would take me seriously."

"Well fine, niggas take you seriously. So seriously that if the time comes to execute and you can't, fear not, you will be executed. Right on the spot, without hesitation. You said you were ready. Well – you'd better be.

"I know what I'm doing," she replied. "I also know that you and I would be perfect for each other. You just need to let the shit happen. It's okay though, I know my day is coming."

"You can keep right on thinking that if you want to. But in the meantime, you better handle your fucking business! Or shall I rephrase, handle me and Ra's business! Not to mention that your first job will be to find a replacement for yourself."

"What? Ain't no replacement for C.C. I thought you knew!"

"Look, if your gonna be handling real work you won't have time to be dealing with no minor shit. You've got two days to get me a new replacement."

"How in the hell am I supposed to get a new person in that short amount of time?"

"I don't know or care but you make it happen. I want Ra to tell me what he thinks of the chick you find."

"It has to be a woman?"

"Damn right! If she's gonna collect bad debts from niggas she needs to be fine! In order to get their attention."

"So does that mean you think I'm fine?"

"Look, I'm not gonna keep doing this Lucy and Ricky shit with you. You want my attention, generate some real money."

The reality was that I might have done C.C. an injustice by having her come by my suite. I just didn't want to be interrupted. As she listened to me and I listened to her. I started to somehow feel a little something for her. It was like a mutual understanding of one another. I mean C.C. was nowhere near ugly. She also had the right amount of clothes on: very little. I had kind-of forgotten how good she looked with her clothes off. I mean, the bitch herself did hair, so you know that stayed the bomb. But what I liked was she wasn't talking crazy for once. And we had a chance to talk about something other than the business. We seldom had the chance to do that. I was usually getting right down to the business at hand when I saw her. But at that moment I saw a different side of C.C. She was a real woman and after we both had a few bottles of MOE, she said she had a hot CD for me to hear. In my head I thought okay, here she go with some loud-ass hip-hop. But I was wrong as hell. She put in some smooth jazz and that really fucked my head up. Of course I didn't let her know it. It wasn't that I wasn't up on the jazz because I listened to the shit all the time, but I never figured C.C. did. By now it was about 12:30, an early evening for street disciples.

I threw a movie in and asked her if she enjoyed the massage.

"Yes, but not half as much as I'm enjoying this evening hanging with you."

We chilled on the sofa. Somehow I drifted off to sleep for a second, and when I opened my eyes her head was on my chest. After the movie, I threw on a smoking jacket, full-length, robe edition. As I went into the bathroom she asked me, "You want a drink?"

I shook it off and replied, "Yea shaken not stirred."

I heard the music change, it was Luther with that anyone who ever loved shit. I couldn't believe it when she called out to me, my dick got hard as shit! To myself I said wait a mother-fucking minute. This is C.C., she works for me. She does hair and collects debts. After that incident with the pistol I really didn't think of her like that. But that was a while ago. This was not the way this shit was supposed to go down. But damn, at that moment she was looking good as shit.

I came out the bathroom and all I saw was C.C.'s body. She had slipped out of the bathrobe and had a spaghetti-strapped bikini top on. I knew things were gonna get ugly right then. Not because of what she was wearing but because of the fact I liked the shit. And at that moment I liked her. She turned around to get the drinks and she had a thong on. There was something in that suite, but I couldn't put my dick on it. There are certain unwritten rules around-the-way. If you and a female both get this certain feeling at the same time, you must fuck. Didn't matter if one of you were married, had a girlfriend or boyfriend or if you were best friends with the woman; once that feeling came down, you had to fuck. This was mandatory!

I was actually feeling a little light-headed at the time. Maybe the MOE was doing a number on me. I think C. C. was tipsy too. I ought to have this glass tested for Ecstasy, I thought to myself. I couldn't deny the fact that we'd always had a decent relationship, but this could fuck up a lot. But FUCK IT, I thought, I'm about to hit this pussy like the devil, shit.

I got a buzz on my phone. It was the bell-boy. I had him on my personal payroll. He reminded me that I had a 3:30am reservation for a helicopter flight over the city. I was due to take Nicky out for a sunrise flight and breakfast. I wondered if I had time to take care of everything. I wasn't sure, but I knew I was gonna scramble C.C.'s eggs if I didn't do anything else that night! We sipped on our drinks, staring at each other. I'm not sure how much time passed, the shit almost seemed like slow motion to me.

"How you feeling," I asked C.C.

"Feeling fine, just like I'm looking."

132

"I know that's right," I said.

I crept across the room and we embraced. The steam was hot, real hot. I started kissing her body and she kissing mine. People in the game seldom tongue kissed anybody unless it was someone you were really into. I laid her down, touching her all over. Everything I felt on her body was soft except her nipples, which were as hard as the bullets in my nine.

"I always knew you were in good shape," she said, caressing my chest. I slid my hands down and ripped her thong off and in the same stroke I threw it across the room. She was rubbing my back with her fingernails. I knew this was gonna get on some old high school shit right then. I still had my robe on. Though at that moment I wish I'd taken it off. I also still had my two shoulder straps on. I slid my hand down her torso and found a nice moist spot. I knew it was on then. I ran my fingers through that puddle one more time and her thighs closed up around my wrist.

"What was wrong?" I asked her.

"Nothing -- you must not have heard me earlier. I told you, before we were just talking about sex. Now I'm talking about you and me. You have far too many women at your disposal as it is. You want to be with me, you're gonna have to respect me."

"Be with you?? Where'd you get that from? We just chillin." I thought about it a second. "Oh, I understand now, you frontin."

"No I'm not frontin B. I want to be with you far more than you want to be with me but you'll have to respect me."

"No problem," I said.

"And what do you mean buy that?'

I was on my feet by then and was wrapping my robe up.

"I said, no problem. Make sure you understand the duties of your promotion. I got other plans for the remainder of the evening. See you at work tomorrow afternoon."

"What other plans? You mean going out with that bitch Nicky?"

"That who? -- What?"

"B, I want to be with you it's just …"

"You'll be with me tomorrow afternoon…at work."

I went to the bathroom. When I came out she was gone. I think that shit worked out best. I couldn't believe that chick fronted like that. Plus I could see the little tension she was showing for me dealing with other women. If she had low tolerance for that, she definitely was not the chick I needed to be boning on the side, or at all for that manner. I couldn't believe I almost slipped like that. I was definitely getting that glass tested for Ecstasy. Getting ready for my flight with Nicky, I'd come to a crossroads. I needed some new information, or maybe some old info.

A Word From The Streets!

The next several months I felt things were going okay, but my head was not really in the game. Not as far as moving forward meant. For the most part, I just saw all of the negatives. It was like I hated what was going on. The fact that Ace had been so in love with the game was not ever thought of as a bad thing to me. But now, I felt like I was the reason that he loved it so much. I had taken him in and given him the opportunity to see real money. He was of age now; the choices he made would be his own. The thing was, I knew what I had to do. I just couldn't bring myself to commit to it. In the Bible, I read that John says, the evil that I don't want to do, I commit; but the good that I want to do, I do not. That's about how I was feeling at the time. I saw Ra and I looked at Tino, they seemed to be loving every moment of this. The multiple chicks, the jewelry, cars, popularity, status and overall juice. I mean that was cool but we had been experiencing that for years, this was nothing new.

C.C. was doing okay and Pam was even holding things down with the girls with no problem. I had only one more goal I needed to hit. That was to get with John Bronson. I wanted to take his place. When this all started he was big and he still at the moment was big as shit. I had to talk to Ra and see what his take was on the whole thing. Part of me wanted the fuck out, but the other part of me wanted to be the biggest there ever was in the game. But as I rewound the tape, I realized that had been the thing to take down every gangster who ever lived. At least the ones I know about. I felt like I needed to get with old Swanson. He'd given me good advice in the past. I was determined to not be just another clown who came and went.

I wanted to tell Nicky what I was going through. I also knew that if a woman saw you were not certain about what you were doing, they tended not to follow you. So talking seriously about getting out and then talking about locking horns with JB would not go over well with Nicky.

I couldn't help wishing I could go to Joe or Kalliq about this shit, but them cats weren't prepared for that. Leek was back in the game for the long haul, whether he wanted to admit that shit to himself or not. He was never gonna be able to go back to making minor figures. Not after making what he'd been making on them pool tables. Plus he was making the money doing what the fuck he loved, not washing dishes at no hospital.

As far as Joey went, he was trying to entertain the thought of us getting out. Which is really where my head was, but he had all those family ties which I didn't think he'd be able to break. Plus, his ass was smarter than most but still young and possibly just going through that first set of cold feet that a cat goes through when you really start stacking true paper.

What the fuck was I up against? I guess it was the plight of all of those who had reached the apex of the game. I went to take a walk through the neighborhood, figured I'd see Swanson somewhere. But he was nowhere to be found. Finally, I stumbled on this cat.

"Yo Swanson what's been up?"

"Your income young B, least that's what I hear."

"You know it ain't never been like that between you and me."

"I can't tell youngster, I don't ever see you around that much anymore."

"Well you know how it is Swan, I got a lot of people counting on me."

"Counting on you or counting for you?"

"What you mean by that shit?"

"Man don't play dumb with me, you'd better know what's being said about you and that crew of yours."

"I'll tell you what, you let me buy you a fifth and you tell me what you've been hearing."

"I've got my own cheese -- but we can still talk"

Swanson? With his own cheese? Somehow that didn't add up.

"Where you getting money from Swan?"

"Never you mind, just know that things are changing for old Swanson."

"I heard that!"

As we walked off, I could feel all eyes on us but that was typical. I seldom came out to the blocks anymore. Most cats in my position would be walking around with bodyguards and shit, but fuck that, I thought, these motherfuckers don't control my moves. The thing that stood out in my mind though was that cats were looking at Swanson too. At first I didn't catch the shit but after awhile I started seeing it. Plus I noticed that Swan was not in his usual bum gear. Cat had on a clean new jean suit, fresh sneakers, a Kangol hat. Not to mention a ring on one finger and a fresh shave.

"So what's the skinny Swanson?"

"Well, first, everybody's wondering when you're gonna try your hand at some of Big John's territory?"

"Who the fuck is Big John?"

"That's right, your ass might not remember when niggas first started calling John 'Big John', but that's what we have always called his ass, 'Big John Bronson'. His territory is the next logical move for you. He's had the same shit all to himself for a long time. And you're expected to get in his pocket. If you don't, niggas is gonna think your ass is soft of scared or something! So what are you gonna do?"

"Well, to tell the truth I hadn't given it as much thought as you obviously have."

"What do you mean you haven't thought about the shit! You'd better get your shit on tight."

"Look, ain't nobody thinking about John's old ass, that nigga ain't been the shit for years, and you know it."

"Who you think you talking to B? I've known your ass for years. You know damn well that you've been wanting to be the biggest thing around for years. You'd better not have changed your mind at this point. It's too late for that shit. All of New York is waiting to see what the fuck your crew's gonna do. The time for you to move is now! And if you don't, your ass won't be shit. I told you a long time ago that this was a game that you have to play for life. Not for the short, medium or long run, for LIFE! For as long as it lasts."

"Come on, JB is an old motherfucker that has had a real long run, what does knocking him out the box have to do with my success?"

"It's not about him or you it's about controlling this place. You're acting like you just got here yesterday. If you don't take him and his crew out, folks will think you're scared of him. It's not about you giving him a pass because he's old. He's not too old to still order a hit on -- your ass. If he's still as sharp as I remember, he probably has some young cats trying to hit your ass right now."

"Listen, I've got bigger things to be concerned with then JB's old ass. I came to you to get some good advice and all you want to do is tell me about some old ass man who ain't no threat to me. Fuck that old ass man!! I'll take his shit down when I get good and ready!"

"Yeah, well, I'll tell you what, your story's touching and all but it sounds like a lie to me. Are you getting sick of this shit? Don't tell me that you don't still want it because it's too late for you to be thinking like that. If you wanted out, the time for that would have been years ago. Your ass is in this shit for life now. You can be king or just some clown who almost climbed the mountain. Those are the choices left for you."

"Yo, I'm glad you took the time to build with the god but I gotta go now."

"Go where? Do what? You wanted to be KINGPIN. Look B, let me tell you this. If you don't do what you need to now, it'll be all over for your ass. And I'm not talking about in a few years neither. It'll only take a hot New York minute for the sharks to figure out that JAWS ain't got no teeth...or ain't hungry no more. You got a bunch of ambitious young cats around you and they're not looking for no laid back leadership! What, you thought the work was over because you've got things under control? You'd better step back and look at that crew you have. You've hand-picked some of the smartest young cats to be assembled in a long time. Each one of them is hungry. Not to mention notoriously violent at times. If they start feeling like you aren't taking them to the obvious next challenges, they will get bored and bounce. And if they do that you will be their first target."

"Wait a damn minute Swan, what are you trying to say to me?"

"I'm telling you that you're at the top of a tidal-wave and you've got to ride this thing into the beach or drown in the water cause you're too far out to casually swim back. I've been watching you put this together and you've done an excellent job, but now there are too many killers on the payroll for you to not keep them busy! And in order to keep a killer busy you have to keep him killing! So this is no time to sharpen your negotiation skills or even begin to start to show any weakness. You've got these cats all worked into a lather. They know that they are part of the most powerful crew on the streets right now and the city has not seen anything like this in years. For them to not forge forward into Big Johns territory would be foolish and suicidal!"

"I don't see JB making no moves."

"Because you don't see it don't mean it's not happening. I'm just telling you don't wait until it's in your face. By the time you see it coming it may be too late."

"Well look, I may need to talk to you again, where've you been hanging at?"

"Oh I've been here and there, just handling things."

"Sounds kinda vague Swanson. How do I hundred percent get a hold of your ass?"

"Well…you can always hit me on the hip B"

"What? When did you get a pager"

"I've had one for a while now.

"Oh, I see, so what's the number?"

As he ran the math down to me I still didn't put the shit together. I told him what my code would be, and he said, "I know the code B."

I should have put something together right there but it took me a minute. Finally, while I was driving off the shit hit me. Swanson was working for me. All the people in my employ knew my code. This was so that if I called, they then knew to respond immediately. I didn't care how far down the totem pole, they all knew my code: 777. All of this suddenly added up. The new clothes, the haircut, having his own dough, even not being in the spots that he used to frequent when he had nothing. This cat was working again. The places he normally hung out in were on Young Bleed's route. Figured I'd make a few calls and find out who put product in this cats hands. Swanson has been using drugs or drinking liquor for years, and nobody in their right mind would give this cat any work. But before I did any of that, I needed to talk to Ra and see what his take was on this John Bronson thing.

I called Ra from my car phone and was not surprised when he told me he was fucking at the time. "Look, when you get done let me know; I need to talk to you about something important."

"I'll call you as soon as I finish up here," promised Ra.

About two hours later, I got a call from Ra. By this time I was back at the Menz Club. He was talking fast and out of breath.

"What the hell is wrong with you Ra? You sound like you've been running hard or something? Where the fuck you at?"

He said he was up on Convent and St. Nick, to which I asked him what was up.

"Get over here right now. Wait, one second though, don't come B, send a car and a few hard hitters."

"What the hell's going on Ra?"

"Send a car and you meet me at the suite in the Waldorf in three hours."

"Ra, look…" CLICK! He hung the phone up.

I wasn't sure exactly what was up, but I knew he needed my help. I made two calls and had three cars of my street soldiers meet Ra at that corner. It took only moments to get to the place Ra had told me he was at. When I got there I saw nothing. I told the driver to circle the block and had the other cars do the same thing, but in different directions. I happened to look in the ally and I saw something. It was Ra. This cat was leaning out of the alley with his .45 out. I called him to the car. He jumped in and I signaled for the other cars to dissipate in different directions.

"Damn Ra, what's all this?"

"The shit with the bitch was a set-up."

"A set up? Who the fuck would have the balls to try to rob your wild ass?"

"Man I know a set up when I see one. When I came down from the building there was more than a few motherfuckers waiting on my ass."

"Recognize any of them?"

"Yeah. I've seen one of them before. But the niggas is old. They ain't got no business even in this part of town."

"Wait a second, I called you to see what the fuck your thoughts were on taking down some of JB's business. And before we can even talk about the shit you telling me that some old clowns tried to hit you out here, on fucking Convent? Is that where you remember seeing this old cat from, being with JB?"

"You know it! I saw this nigga all hugged up with a few chicks at the bar at the player's ball in Chicago last year. I remembered the guy because he was with JB and that crew that be on his side of town. I remember telling Tino that them niggas was still doing swell to be so old.

"Now that you mention the shit I do remember you saying something about this old nigga with a beard and shit. Tino have you been seeing this cat around?"

"No but I do remember when Ra said that about him at the ball. Them niggas is a little old, but at the ball they had wild juice! Okay fuck it that's it, this shit is war. These motherfuckers have got to bleed over this shit."

"Fuck you talking about Tino your ass don't give no orders or start no wars. We gonna see just the best way to handle the shit. Ra what you got on deck for the next few hours?"

"Nothing now. Had some more pussy to go and get but fuck that, a nigga don't feel like fucking now. I want somebody's head on the floor!"

"So tell me just how the fuck this whole shit went down."

"I was coming out the building and motherfuckers, was out there with heat."

"Did any shots get dropped?"

"Hell yeah!! I set that shit off directly. I wasn't waiting for a motherfucking second. I shot two of them clowns and I know their asses is dead!"

"How the fuck are you so sure that they're dead?"

"I saw one of them holding his guts and trying to get back into the car. You and I both know that don't nobody live after a stomach shot unless they're right outside the doctor's office. The other one caught a bad one in the melon."

"Well that will be the first thing that we will half to address. I'll call Tammy, she works at the hospital and she can tell me if anyone got admitted with gunshots to the midsection or head trauma."

"Wait. Why are you doing that shit? Let's just go and hit a few of his guys and call it a day when we kill his sister and moms."

"No, because, that's what they're expecting. JB knows damn well that you and me are the principle players in this shit. Now don't take this wrong but if he wanted you dead, you would have been dead. Look at all of the guns that you said were on you. There is no way that you could have out gunned that many niggas. He probably knew that your ass would smell a rat and dip from the shit or call for some backup. I think that cat just wanted to see first hand how fast our reaction time was and how well our organization is. Besides, if I had to hit a young, strong, active dude I doubt that I would send an aging crook. If I wanted him dead I would send the best of my youngsters."

"Oh, that's what he want to see? I say let me go and show him just how fast this heat hit his ass."

"Look Ra this is no time for us to act all wild and predictable. I need that smart crafty-ass Ra that I started this shit with, not that wild juvenile Ra that you've been showing everybody recently."

"Wait, what do you mean by that shit?"

"Come on man, you know you and Tino have been doing everything but setting this place on fire."

"Yeah — and so what. You've been running around with your head up your ass for a minute too."

"My head up my ass?"

"Yes nigga, your head up your ass, like you were trying to snort your own balls or something!"

"You name it! I've been keeping this thing together while your ass has been having one big party with Tino!"

"Look at you? Sounding like a bitch, like a chick that just lost her favorite girlfriend or some shit."

"Look, we both been fucking up, now knowledge that."

"Indeed god, that's true. But now we gonna put this old Nigga in his fucking place, a casket."

"True, but how we do this is gonna have to be some well thought, well-planed shit. I'm sure that the streets is watching extra close on this one."

"One thing's for sure, I don't think it should be you or me that puts this piece of work in."

"What makes you say that Ra?"

"Look I didn't want to say anything in front of the others but I saw a few other cats out there and they wasn't no fucking locals. They was some other-motherfuckers, from Chi–Town. And I'm not talking about no pimps. These motherfuckers is killers all day. That's what they were doing in Chicago, hitting some big time nigga for another nigga from East St. Louis. They are all about money. The highest bidder is who achieves their services."

"Did you hit one of them sharpshooters?"

"Na. The funny thing is that they never shot a round."

"Wait, all this shit was going on and they never busted a shot? That's not good at all."

"Why you say that god?"

"Man, that means these cats is some real pro's. And they ain't wasting no shots that don't connect."

"Are you deaf? That's what I was trying to tell you. When I saw these niggas in Chi-Town they was at it like Rakim and them, straight NO-JOKE!

"Then how the hell did you find out about what kinda time they were on?"

"Well, I was at this little thug orgy; this bitch started running her mouth about all of the big-timers that she'd been with and some of the wild stuff they had her do. She mentioned that that same crew had hired her and her friends one night and they got on some old bestiality shit!"

"What? That's sex with small animals involved and shit, ain't it?"

"Yeah, but anyway I found myself alone with her and she told me about all of them clowns. Whenever I think about the shit I'm glad that you suggested that Tino and I go out there because I did learn a lot of new shit and I did see some niggas I haven't seen since jail. I can say one thing I did pickup was that nowadays niggas don't get no local guns to do their work. If we gonna get some guys, they need to be from out of town to."

"You're right Ra. When they're done with the work we can send their asses packing and don't have to worry about them snitchin or nothin."

"Well, that's part of it. But I was thinking more along the lines of you and me being the only ones who they deal with and when it's over with we could just kill 'em, you know?"

"Yeah, you're right. What was I thinking! Well you up for the shit?"

"Hell yeah! We take this shit all the way to the grave; or to paradise."

Problems on St. Nick & Convent

"C.C., Pam, what the fuck are you all doing arguing in the fucking Menz Club?"

"This bitch right here has got to have her ass kicked!"

"Pam what are you talking about?"

"This bitch beat up one of my girls! And God as my witness she gonna get her ass kicked or cut, I mean it Ra!"

"Wait, tell me what the fuck is going on first."

"I'm trying to have a staff meeting and in come this funky pussy talking about somebody done parked in her space one time too many! I told her we would address that in a minute but she couldn't wait! She asked who was driving the red Camry and Corey said it was hers. Before I could even tell the girl to apologize, C.C. was all over the woman. I ran over there to stop the shit and she's steady hitting the girl in the face! Now, her tits ain't big as two golf balls and she really don't have the ass for the job, but the girl had the face of an angel. That's been what was getting the tricks to pay her. She looks like her face done been put through a meat grinder now! It will be at least two maybe three weeks before she can work again. Do you know how much money that is? I ain't gonna have Brisco talking shit to me or you threatening to kick my ass behind the numbers being down. Saying to me, 'you know it ain't but one way out' and shit. Plus it's the point of the shit; she disrespected me. I was holding a meeting and all of my staff saw this happen. No, fuck that, she got to have her ass kicked for this!"

"Fuck you and your phony ass staff, a bunch of stinking ass cum-swallowing bitches, now you want me to show you some respect? Suck my douche water through a straw Pam; clown bitch!"

"C.C. I was going to give you a chance to tell your side but I've got the feeling that I have heard about as much of the truth as I'm gonna get. Bleed, get B on the phone."

"Ra you gonna call Pin over this little shit? If it were me I would--"

"Well it ain't you; so shut the hell up and get the god on the phone. I hate dealing with these stupid-ass bitches. The rest of you girls get the fuck out, except C.C. and Pam. If I had my way all of you would be on the strip selling this shit the old fashioned way."

"Like your moms," whispered C.C.

BOOM! "Damn it Ra you trying to kill the girl!" said a suddenly concerned Pam.

"You motherfucking right, say another word Pam and your ass is next! I see I need to do some chin checking! Hey kid, did you get the god on the horn or what?"

"Yea he's----"

"What the fuck is going on in this joint?" I hollered. "And Ra, how'd C.C. get on the floor? Pam what the fuck are you doing hovering over her? WHAT THE HELL JUST HAPPENED IN THIS CLUB? I can't get up the stairs without a few of the girls telling me that one of the girls got beat up by a trick, I see some chick that looks like she just went at it with a Mack truck. I come into the conference room and C.C. is laid on the floor, knocked the fuck out and this kid is blowing my hip up with 911 pages and shit! Now I'm gonna ask this shit one more time: what the hell is going on in this club?"

"These is your bitches. I was not going to get involved with the shit really. It looks to me like they had some sort of disagreement. Pam was about to tax C.C.'s ass or they was about to have one hell of a brawl in this spot. Your girl *Consuelo* couldn't keep her mouth shut so I helped her ass out."

153

"Ra you knocked C.C. out?"

"With one punch, my man Ra still got that touch."

"Tino relax with that shit, I'm trying to settle this shit."

"Settle what this bitch has been slipping out of her mouth with little shit for a minute now. She needed to be reminded who bleeds once a month and who don't."

"O.K. Ra it's done let's get down to the real business at hand. Ra I'm asking you to pardon yourself towards C.C."

"Yeah, all right. It's done."

"Thank you Ra. C.C. are you alright?"

"Hum, what? "

"Pam how is she?"

"Her ass won't die. She'll be fine in a few. But B you ain't gonna say nothing else about what he did?"

"Pam are you sticking up for C.C., who you yourself were about to get into it with?"

"No"

"Well then, it's settled. Look, we might as well talk about this shit right now! We're at a cross in the road. I am involving you all for a very specific reason. This next challenge that we face will propel us into the highest level of the major leagues. I feel that you should all at least know what the hell is going on before we get started with the topic. I want you to understand that you are all adult criminals at this point. Your numeric age does not matter. You have been in or around the game long enough to know that you can die in a moment's notice. Ra and myself have gone to great lengths to make sure that for the most part few of us are dead or rotting in a cell someplace. For us to take these next few steps will be the deciding factor for some of you and quite certainly, death for some as well. You have made fast money, as well as good money, but if you want that never-work- again status this will be the move."

"Yeah, and if you pussy's want to go out like some soldiers, now is the time or you can act like a bunch of hoe-ass faggots," added Ra, after which I continued.

"Okay, the topic is John Bronson. "

"His ass has got to go."

"C.C. why are you saying that?" asked Ra.

"Well, he has some territory that could be ours and I don't see any reason that what he has should not be what we have."

I opened the platform further.

"Tino, your thoughts."

"Well, I think personally that we should have been touched his ass, but if now is the time I say let's get at it. Plus I got personal beef with the old man for trying to set my man up."

"Pam, your thoughts?"

"Oh, now yawl want my opinion, usually I'm just supposed to be some *old-ho-bitch*."

"Well now is your time to speak, you got something to lend to this or not?"

"Well, yeah, I ain't scared or nothing but the last time a crew tried something against this guy they all ended up dead. I'm not talking about fucked up or in jail, I mean dead. It was not just the head people, I mean all of that crew was dead! So if you do something to this guy you had better be prepared to take it all the way. Cause he won't stop until everybody is dead!"

"Okay, now that you're done ridding his balls, can we hear the plan," barked Ra at Pam. "Scared Bitch."

"Well the plan is very simple, we start killing his people off one at a time. But in order to set it up we will have to kill his right hand man first."

Ace chipped in: "Hey Pin, look if we can get close enough to kill his right hand man why don't we just kill him?"

"I understand your thinking kid, but first off it will not be easy to get to his right hand man and I don't want him dead just yet."

C.C. suddenly spoke out. "Now B, JB comes from a different era of doing things. I'm not even sure who his right hand man is?"

"You're correct C.C., that's gonna be where Pam will come into play. I want you to find out who the fuck he trusts and where they can be found," I ordered.

"Wait a Goddamn minute. This ain't none of my doing. I work the girls I don't do the kind of shit that you're talking about. Why don't you get C.C. to do the shit, that's her specialty- not mine. You said I'd be working the bar "B," not nothing else?"

"WELL HE CHANGED HIS MIND BITCH," yells Ra. "YOU JUST FUCKING PERFORM AND DON'T LET THIS CREW DOWN!"

At this point Tino is in the floor with laughter.

I had not responded because, again, though I did not like the delivery, Ra was correct. I did feel that something should be said. I took a long pull on my cigar and responded:

"Look Pam, it would be possibly expected to send C.C. But I'm sending the right person for the job."

"Is you ass in or out?" yells Tino.

"Quiet Tino," I order, before continuing. "Now look here Pam, your ass didn't have any problem spending the money this crew put together, so get out there and handle this business. You should have no problem coming up with this info. Your girls can easily get close to one or two of his people and let me know where his man lives and all of his activities. I need to know all about this guy."

"I feel you god," adds Tino, "That's what I'm talking about. We need to get rid of any dead weight that might be lingering around."

"This time I think that Tino is right, we need to assess who the fuck means to get it all and who is just going along for the ride. Pam you've got a week to get me the info that I need."

"And what exact info is that?"

"Pam I need to know where his top people reside. Mainly the places they frequent at night. I also want to know his pay schedule. It's important. Tino you so hyper to kill this cat I want you to tell me everything about his movements and his family. I don't want your ass to be going around asking questions either!"

"Well how the hell am I supposed to find out anything without asking around?" says Pam.

"Tino, you're a pretty new face in town; a few people on our side of town might know you but basically you are a new face. That will work in our favor if you play it right. If you go around asking a bunch of corny questions it could alert this cat that we are up for a strike, understand?"

"Yeah, that shit makes sense, but we all got other duties to attend, how the fuck are we supposed to handle following cats and all of this Colombo shit and do our normal business?"

"THIS IS YOUR NORMAL BUISNESS!! YOU MOTHERFUCKERS IS CRIMINALS, AIN'T NO NINE TO FIVE IDEOLOGIES HERE! THAT'S PART OF THE FUCKING PROBLEM! NIGGAS GETTING LAZY! WORKING ON

BANKERS-HOURS AND SHIT. THIS MOTHERFUCKER JUST TRIED TO HIT MY MAN AND YOU'R E GONNA DO JUST WHAT THE FUCK I SAY TO GET THIS OLD CLOWN OR I WILL SYSEMATICALLY START KILLING YOU MOTHERFUCKERS MYSELF!"

And at that, the muthafuckin meeting was adjourned.

On The Job

"Yo Ra what's up."

"Hey Tino how's it going down?"

"It's cool but look what was up with your man the other day. He was talking about killing niggas off and shit, what up with that shit!"

"Well you know how it is, emotions run high between me and the god so I wouldn't take the shit personally but the nigga is serious about having JB take the dirt nap though. How's your search going?"

"I've been watching the guy but I've got to say he's a hard old man to follow. He does a lot of moving about and he has a gang of cats on the payroll. I still have not found out exactly where he sleeps. So far, he hasn't slept in the same bed twice. But I can say this, the nigga never sleeps alone. He always has a honey or two with him when night falls."

"Is he fucking theses chicks or what?"

"Look Ra, I just told you that the old man was hard as hell to put a bead on. Now you asking me about his sex life. I thought you cats wanted to know his whereabouts so we could place a hit or something not sit and worry about what brand of condom this guy uses."

"You funny Tino, but look I've got to make my rounds and check on Bleed & Pam to see how they're handling things. I'll speak with you around seven. Peace."

"True indeed god I'll see you in the god hour"

"Pam how are you doing with that info for "B?"

"I'm coming along pretty well, it's actually a little easier than I thought to get a hold of this guy."

"That's funny I talked to Tino and he said that the man was hard to follow and difficult to catch up with."

"He's probably not lying from his standpoint. He's a young muscular nigga, who looks like some trouble. I, on the other hand, am a sexy diva who looks like a good time."

"Don't tell me this old man's got the hots for your old ass."

"Fuck you Ra, he isn't as old as you motherfuckers think he is. He's still got eyes good enough to see this good thing."

"O.K. you've got his attention, what else do you have that will be helpful in nailing this cat down?"

"Not much just yet, I know that he has a few kids that live in Boston somewhere. I also know that the negro keeps a forty- five on his hip and a .22 revolver in his boot. Not to mention that he always wears boots.

"How'd you find out about the boot action? You, fucking him?"

"No, but one of my girls is dating his nephew and he told her that behind a motorcycle accident years ago the man always wears boots."

"Cool that's good work Pam, I'll tell B what you've found. Look, stay close to your pager for the next few hours. I'll be hitting you soon.

"Why don't you just hit me on the cell phone?"

"For now we're all going on limited use of then damn phones until we get a few things under control. You can use the phone but watch what the hell you say and make sure that you know who the hell you're talking to. Shit, that's my pager going off, I'll get at you later Pam."

"What's up B, where are you?" asks Ra.

"You know; Knowledge, Knowledge, Power god. I'll see at half pass 'build' hour."

"True indeed god it's done!"

I suddenly see Ra coming up on 115th at 8:30, just as we'd discussed using our Five Percent codes we used to when we were much younger. Weird thing was, Ra had a big smile on his face, I could tell he had some news that he wanted to tell me bad.

"What's the science god?"

"Knowledge, Understanding; Culture Freedom," I respond.

"Ah yeah, I see the god is still sharp with the science!"

"Enough with the reminiscing. What you got for me on the information side of things?"

"Look I spoke with Tino and Pam and they're doing good work. Pam knows what type of heat this cat keeps on him and Tino is doing well with keeping up with the cat. He says that he keeps a girl or two with him at night."

"So what he plays the streets. How's that going to get us under this guy?"

"Look B, you have got to play it cool and let me do my thing on this one. The only thing that the street needs to see from you is business as usual, which for right now is low visibility. I'm not gonna let a stone go unturned. I've instructed a few of the crew to lay off the cell phone use like you said. I also think it's a good idea for us to continue with the same communication that we've been using. This way we know our phones aren't being hit on. And even if they are, they can't make out what we are up to."

"Ra that's good work that Tino and Pam are putting in but I'm telling you, I've got a funny feeling that this motherfucker needs to be dead now."

163

"I agree, but you said we should be smart and that was good info."

"Have you got any particular way that you want this nigga to go?"

"Ra why are you asking me that now? We don't really know enough to strike yet and you want my opinion on how he should go?"

"Well he did try to kill you and I know I was next. But the fact remains, he did make an effort to put you under. So, I felt that it should be your call. Don't worry I want this clown to die so the whole world will know without a doubt we are running things."

Too Many Chefs

"What are you saying they've got to come to court? Damn Mr. A, I was counting on you making sure we could handle this without actual court appearances!"

"I'm the best at what I do, but you can't expect me to work miracles. You are paying me because you know that I have your best interest at heart. I've never let you down before so why question the tactics now. The charges are stiff and some of these guys are going to have to do some time. You are not a couple of kids just raising a little dust. You are known criminals who run a virtual empire one that the local cops can't seem to capture with enough evidence to make charges really stick! That alone has some people in very high places holding a hard-on for you. You have been more that fortunate but all things have a price. Now you and that character Ra can make some tough choices or let things take whatever course they're going to take. But I'm telling you, somebody is going to jail on this one, and I don't mean for the short run. I can pretty much predict that two or more will go in all day -- and a few will do ten or more! Not to mention that thing, with the woman, that everybody apparently knew worked for you. That foolishness made the front page of the Post and it still is on the top-ten unsolved cases. That connection to you and your group doesn't help things."

"Look Pam was grown and you and I both know who killed her Mr. A."

"Yes we both know, but it's your job to keep this jive time gangster shit out the papers. When a relatively young woman gets beaten to death with a bull-whip and her fucking tits get cut off, you can bet the news crews are going to have a ball with the shit!"

"Listen Mr. A, you must be listening to the papers yourself if you think I can stop shit like that from happening. I've got my power, but even that has limits. I didn't want that to happen to Pam, but what was I supposed to do? She was working -- and in our work that stuff happens."

"That stuff happens? Is that your reasoning for this shit that has gone on in this city over the last six months? You and that asshole JB have used this city as your own little sandbox and you've both been playing army men with the place! The problem is the people are real and the death has been more than the Mayor is willing to write off as just some small gang problem! It's organized crime and that's why they have special prosecutors involved as well as special investigators. I'm telling you this is chess on a higher level. You will not be able to keep playing, unless you become more willing to lose a few pawns. You can't save theses people and yourself. You have a substantial amount of money. I know this for a fact. And you always were a smart guy. Why don't you consider just letting this go. Just let this be what it is. I know that your *compadr'e* Ra has lots of cash as well. If it's not out of concern for him that you stay, then why not just go? Is it a woman? Is it that kid Havolice? What could possibly keep you here to try and save the non-savable? You know what? I'm done. You want me to defend these people, I'll do it and I'll do my best to get them off. But I've told you what I think the outcome is going to be. And that is my professional opinion. You on the other hand stand quite a chance at making it out of here. But that asshole Ra is going to do something stupid, it's just a matter of time. That's without you to keep him on track. He is like Tyson without Cus D'Amato! Just a matter of time."

"Mr. A, I appreciate the words. Really I do. But I started this and I know what has got to go on. I'm paying you a lot of money and I have a personal CPA who is going to remain anonymous to you. They will pay as your need arises. I want you to defend all of my people as you would your own. Okay?"

"No problem, I've always responded to finance but remember I told you that some time would have to be served. There is really no way around that. I would not be offended if you wanted to get a second legal opinion."

"Look Mr. A I have never questioned your ability. If I needed a second opinion I wouldn't need you."

"Well I appreciate the fact that you trust me but you seem to not be accepting the fact that some will do time very well."

"Mr. A, have you ever done any time?"

"Brisco you know better than that."

"That's why you speak on the concept of prison for long periods of time with such a flip attitude. Do you remember how you felt when your son was in the House of Pain? Do you remember how helpless you felt when he needed your help and your abilities were useless to assist him. It was me that was able to do what seemed to be the impossible. I need you to now go out and do that same impossible for me. For some of these individuals the penitentiary might as well be the death penalty. So yes, if it seems to not be business as usual for me to accept with ease that members of my group are going to spend the rest of their lives in a steel box, then you're right. I'll call you in a few days to find out what the new legal prospects are."

"Brisco, I understand and I will do my very best. I also wanted to tell you this. I'm sure that the Feds are involved in this and I know for a fact that there is a leak in your group."

"What do you mean a leak?"

"I've got a few old friends that work for the Feds and they have told me in the deepest confidence that there is a person in your group who is working with them. Apparently that person is fairly close to the top. Now I'll never tell you how to get things done but I would shut the leak off if I could. I'm sure you understand."

"I think your old friend is just trying to see what you know. I've got some things to tend to, I'll call you in a few days."

"Brisco—I'm serious."

I walked out the room and I knew that Mr. A knew what he was talking about. This just made certain the thoughts I was already having about the crew. I can't go to these cats and tell them that the jail cell is calling. They would definitely start talking and flipping. I needed some pussy from a chick that is for real. I was thinking of calling C.C. My head was so out of whack I didn't even care about the consequences. Nicky was getting further and further away from my mind. She was not going to be able to withstand the storm, I could see that very clearly now. She had the right stuff for me if my life was different, but she could not go the distance on the course I currently traveled. I needed for now a real street chick with some good sense. The more I thought about what I needed, the more I realized the Nicky was on her way out, and C.C. was looking better and better.

C.C. had lost some weight in recent months and had really started to embrace some classy ways. She was never bad looking to me but I think that a lot of it was my ego and the fact that I cared what Ra and some of the others thought. Partly, perhaps, because they had seen me with so many starlets and shit. What they didn't see was that them video hoe's, actresses and lawyer types could nag the shit out of you. Not to mention most times they weren't equipped to deal with a real negro. And they also didn't know when to shut the fuck up. But C.C. knew when to let a man be a man, and could also sense a lot of the shit a woman needed to know. I didn't think I could really leave the city with her. But just for the night, she was what the doctor ordered. Fuck it, I decided to shoot past her rest.

"Yo C.C. What's up?"

"Nothing, what's up with you? I thought you and Ra would be out with the Young Bleed having fun."

"Why do you say that?"

"Well you've been spending so much time with JB, the cases and having to watch Tino and now you have your friend Joe here. I just figured you all would be out having fun with some girls for the night."

"All that you said is true, but right now I'm out front your building parking the car. I'm coming up."

"Well if you are coming up you might as well park in the underground parking garage."

"Cool I'll be up in a few."

"Let me ask you this, are you staying long?"

"Well yeah, I have some things to talk to you about"

To Talk About The Game

"Look Joe, let's take a trip for a few long ticks. I've got some ideas I think you might be interested in."

"Well I'm wit it man but…"

"What's the problem, Crillz?"

"Look, you got more than a few of your team coming up on trials. You and Ra are handling things like business as usual. I mean them trials could go either way. You cats must know something that the rest of us don't, but-Fuck it! You know me B, I'm always down for it. But let me say this, I know how you and that 'tick' shit goes, so how should I pack and what's the weather gonna be."

"Now you buggin. I was just gonna show you some property I had down south and see if you'd be down to check out some of the locals. You know, just chill. Grab a few honeys and play Daniel Boone."

"Okay, whatever you say. All I know is that I've heard about you and these road trips; it always starts off as something simple and then somebody comes back with a story to tell."

"Look I'm bouncing in the A.M. you coming or what?"

"Yeah what the hell, I'm in. What time you coming through?"

"I'll be at your crib at 4am, so be ready!"

"Cool B, I'll be up."

4 a.m. on the button and Joe was right where he said he'd be: Standing out front his building.

"You got your bags in the back straight?"

"Yeah, B, let's boogie kid. I was bustin it up with these shorties last night and I'm hung out and tired as hell. I'm a hit this comma real fast."

"Go ahead get some sleep, I got a lot on my mind and the highway will give me some time to think."

I still at that moment had no idea what it was that Swanson had been trying to tell me. I kept repeating the shit to myself but it made no sense. I kept thinking about Pam and what she must have been thinking those last few moments of her life. She had been a very loyal worker. I wanted to just write the shit off, like Ra had done, but I couldn't hide from myself. It was fucking with me. I had to figure out why. It didn't make sense for her to be bothering me. She was dead and people always died in this game. I'd seen plenty of this shit before. Maybe it was some of the last few things she said about not wanting to take the job of getting close to J.B. I didn't know, but I knew I couldn't get it out my mind. I was sick of the whole thing at this point. The out-smarting the police, the street-scene, the constant shorties wanting to be me or thinking that they could replace me. I was starting to suspect a glass of water had a motive against me. Still, there was a leak or a snitch somewhere in this unit. If I didn't figure out what the hell was going on soon my ass would wind up dead or in jail. I've looked at all the angles and I just didn't see it. I couldn't go to anybody for assistance because really, everybody was a suspect. At this point the only person who was beyond reproach was Ra. He and I started this together and we both stood to loose if either one of us took a loss.

Sometimes just getting away from the city was just what I needed to figure things out. No use in me calculating the gains, I took a different approach, and looked at what everybody loses.

Joey Crillz and I got down to the country and I saw my shorty.

"Yo Joe, check my little country shorty out."

"Yeah she look like a pretty *thorough* jo'n. Damn, she let you call her country?"

174

"No not in public. She always corrects me and says that she's 'southern not country- there is a difference'. I be like, whatever. You know, I never really took the time out to consider honey. Through it all she's been a pretty constant figure and she don't care about the lifestyle because she doesn't know about it. She's country but that's cool cause she be cookin for a nigga."

"Wait, you mean to tell me that this joint has no idea who your ass is or what the fuck you're into?"

"Na, Joey, she don't know shit."

"Look B, You know that I'm the last one to step into your shit when it comes to business. But if you think that because we had to drive forever to get here that this joint don't know who the hell you are -- you are tripp'in. Cause kid, the shit is known."

"Look, I've known this shorty since it was barely legal for us to have sex. If she knew I would know she knew. Feel me."

"Yeah, all right. I'll let you tell it. Look, where the hell are we anyway? I fell asleep in the truck and I feel like I've been asleep for a week."

"You damn near have been. We're in N.C."

"Fucking Carolina??"

"Yeah, this is one of my little getaway spots I've been coming here for years. This is my spot to ruff it in."

"Ruff-it, you wasn't bullshitting this shit look like it's a hundred years old. Where the hell is Abe Lincoln and the cherry tree?"

175

"Once you get inside you'll be all right"

"Goddamn kid, did I say Abe Lincoln! Where the fuck is Fred Flintstone? This kitchen is from the Stone Age. The Damn stove is actually - a stove. You expecting me to eat off of this shit! The Goddamn stove has rust on it. Look I got love but fuck this Hansel and Grettrel shit, get me on the first thing smoking back to Philly."

"Yo relax, I know the shit is a shock to your fucking system but that is why I like the spot, it's low profile. Far from that shit we exist in. I'm gonna go out and have my shorty round up a shorty for you and the shit will be peace. Why do you care about the cooking arrangements? I don't see you doing any cooking anyway."

"Now you know what? You're damn right about that shit! I know you've got the original Aunt Jemima locked in some little country version of the control room. You'd better let her ass out so she can cook for us."

"Nigga your buggin. Go take a shower and get some rest. I'll wake you up when the shorties are on they way."

At that moment I concealed my inquisitive nature. But what Joe had just said had probably changed my life forever. It was like a light bulb just went off in my mind. I had been racking my brain trying to figure out what the hell I was doing wrong and it was right there in that rural setting that the truth had revealed itself to me.

The girls came by a few hours later and all went as expected. The shorty that Billie had with her was sharp. This was to be expected. I had told her that Joe was a picky nigga and to bring a shorty that was fly and good looking. I think her name was Tammy or something. It didn't really matter, I knew Joe was gonna come up with the ass. I think she said she had a job cooking in a little greasy spoon somewhere. This was perfect because when you had a couple shorties who could fuck, cook and who didn't run they mouths about a lot of dumb shit, you were guaranteed to have a good time.

It had been three days and we had not left the crib yet. I thought Joe might have been getting a little restless but Tammy was keeping him quite busy. I was thinking about my situation and I was getting more clarity towards the shit as the days passed. I did want to take some time to ask Billie a few things though.

"Yo Billie, let me talk to you for a few ticks."

"Sure baby. What's up"

"Look, let me ask you this, do you know how long we've been messing around with each other?"

"Yeah, I know how long, since my 18th birthday. I remember because I couldn't wait. I wanted you to be my first and you were."

177

"Whatever, maybe I was your first orgasm but not your first. I'm not going through that shit with you again. What I really want to know from you is - what do you feel for me?"

"What do you mean? You've always been real cool but I don't sweat you with how I feel because I know how it goes with you."

"What do you mean how it goes with me?"

"I know that you can have your way with a lot of females and I know that you have a lot of money"

"What makes you say that?"

"I always see you in nice cars and I never hear you mention money. To me that's a sign of a person who has plenty of money. As far as the girls go, I can see that you're in good shape and you've always been better than just nice looking!"

To be honest I had to put Tammy in her place. At first she thought it was about to be some two-some shit about to happen.

"Now I don't fool myself by trying to claim you or no shit like that," continued Tammy. "But...I do love you. And I'm in love with you. I just don't say anything about it because I know that's not what you're trying to hear; just like I don't mention the drug thing."

"Wait! What drug thing?"

"Please. I don't leave here often but sometimes niggas from the big cities come through here and they all run their mouths.

178

They figure the shit they saying won't matter because we're all supposed to be a bunch of dumb farmers or something. But for real, I see a lot, I just don't say much. It took me a second or two to finally make sense out of the shit. A few years ago my cousin stayed in New York. She got a job as a bartender for a one-night party that some big time roller was throwing for his crew. She said that the guy who threw the party was a real big guy in the streets and he had a real dangerous crew. The thing that set me off was she said that nobody called him by his name, everybody called him KINGPIN. She also said she heard one of his top people call him Brisco. That's when I figured out that you were who you are. I never said anything because I thought it might make you not like me any more."

"Look Billie, I must admit that I did like the fact that you didn't know who I was but I don't think that it would have kept me from dealing with you. I just liked the fact that you never asked me about where I go or how come we don't see more of each other."

"For a long time I wanted to ask you but once I figured out what was happening, I just thought you'd rather be left alone."

"Well one thing is correct, I don't want to spend any time talking with you about some drug shit. But I do want to ask you why you never left this place. You're smart and you could do so much more with your life."

"My mother was old and my father died years ago. But I promised my father I wouldn't leave my mother. I finished college last year and my mother passed a few months after I graduated. I sold the family business and wrapped up all the details. I just have the property to sell to my cousin and then I've got one more thing I'm waiting on. When I take care of that I am leaving."

"I've got to say this, you have done quite a few things that I had no idea about. Talk about hidden lives. Here I am thinking that you just some sexy little country shorty."

" I told you southern not country, there's a difference."

"Know what, you're right because I couldn't see no 'country shorty' pulling off all the work that you've done. I'm gonna give you your props on that shit from now on. It's southern not country."

"It's about time you gave me some credit for something"

"Yo Joe you up yet?"

"Wait a minute, we butterball in this piece."

"Look I got an idea for some fun nigga. Plus you need some fresh air. I'll see you downstairs in 10 minutes. Billie got breakfast going and shit."

"Tammy got plenty of bacon and I'm scrambling her eggs in here. You feel me."

"Yeah okay nigga, I'll see you downstairs when you get done."

An hour later this cat crawling comes downstairs.

"Look I must admit this country shit does have its benefits."

"Oh, so now you liking that little shorty?"

"Nigga what's not to like? She fuck like she mean it. She cooks like the nigga on the cream of wheat box. And like you said, she don't talk about a lot of dumb shit."

"So I take it that you digg'in it out here."

"It's cool for a little getaway spot. I knew the shit was gonna be cool if you had planned it out. It's definitely free of distractions. What's up with this fresh-air shit you were talking about?"

"I've got the shotgun and the rifle loaded up, I figured we'd go out and do a little hunting."

"HUNTING! Nigga you wasn't bullshitting when you said play Daniel Boon, were you?"

"Well we probably won't see much but it's an activity that gets niggas out of the house for a few. Plus the way you've been going at it, Tammy's ass probably needs some time to recuperate."

"Shit I could use some recoup time too. Fuck it I'm down."

"I'm gonna go start these ATV's up."

"Oh nigga, you didn't say that you had the four wheel joints! Now I'm really with that shit."

Two hours later we were deep in the woods, but still on my property.

"Yo, nigga, this laying in the leaves is offending my inner city stance on life," complained Joe. "Plus I'm finding that these Timbs I'm wearing ain't keeping my feet as dry and warm as the guy on the commercial looked."

"You keep running your mouth, of course we ain't gonna hit shit. With you scaring off all the prey. I thought you was a better shot than what you showing me?"

"What do you mean, I'm a better shot than you?"

"She-it I can't tell. Pick something out and I'll hit the shit."

"Alright that birds nest over there."

"Cool."

"Wait B, you using a shotgun nigga, use this rifle I've been using."

"That's cool you ain't said nothing"

POW! A hit my mark cleanly.

"Now nigga what!"

"O.K. a lucky shot."

"You pick something and I'll hit the shit," claimed Joe.

"Cool that oak over there with the bend in it and the rotten spot. Then hit the tree beside it."

"Nigga what! It's done. Hand me the rifle."

POW! POW! Joe fired the rifle, hitting his mark clean as well. I squinted my eyes up ahead.

"Looks like you missed to me," I said.

"Nigga you are crazy? I hit them shit's dead on. But to make you happy I'm gonna go down there and cut them two rounds out and show them to you. Then I'm going back to the crib. Hold this rifle."

It was as if the temperature had abruptly dropped to single-digit degrees. True-enough, it was cold out there but that wasn't it. It was more the cold, clammy, feeling that was coming from my insides. The snitch, I realized, was Joey Crillz. My trusted friend and compadr`e. I had played ball with Joe during the summer league. I was one of the older kids and he was just a young boy that I took a liking to. He always acted right and always said and did the right thing. Joe always seemed to be just a little more mature than his age. He and I had made smart moves in the game. He had been like a younger brother to me. I'd advised him on a lot of things and ironically he'd given me some good suggestions now and then. His mother was like an aunt to me. His little sister, always sassy, was just that, a little sister to me. But we were grown men now and I couldn't bring myself to accept the truth. That this man, my friend had been the reason for Pam's death and the possible demise of my organization, my crew, my dream.

Joe never wanted anybody in his crib. From the time he came to New York to stay, he'd always be waiting for you out front or at the bodega down the block. His questions were somewhat too curious. His concerns about the upcoming trials and the structure of things all tips that I should have recognized. The fact that Tino, one who has made a living in his city did not really fuck with the cat, was another sign that I should have noticed. His apprehension towards this trip, wanting to know how to dress was another tip. We were upper echelon drug dealers who always bought what we needed when we got there, or at least that how we'd always done it. Why, all of a sudden, did he need an itinerary? And finally, his making mention of the control room in the kitchen also struck a cord. The only people who knew of that room was Ra, who it so happens never truly cared for Joe. Young Bleed who was too scared to tell anyone. And I had never spoken to Joe about that room.

While he was using a knife to pick the rounds out of the oak tree, I slowly took aim with the rifle and shot him in the ankle. I heard him scream out in pain. He was down. As I ran towards him, he thought someone else had shot him and I was coming to his rescue. He still had no idea that I was to go from betrayed friend to bitter executioner.

"Yo, I dropped my knife get me one of those guns so we could kill these clowns that shot me!"

"No need kid." I gestured to tie his hand and as I suspected, he put up a fight. I hit him in the head with the butt of the rifle and he was out cold. I tied him up between two trees. His legs and arms were spread eagle, making him look like a letter X. I waited for him to come too. It was only a few minuets.

"Yo, "B" what the fuck is going on?"

"You tell me Joe. You tell my why the fuck you're snitching out my shit to the Fed's? Tell me why you're talking to me about my control room?"

"Look, I had a runner drop my moms off for a doctor's appointment. He got pulled over the car was hot as hell and he had product in the trunk. The Fed's knew that they couldn't put the shit on me directly, but they could put the shit on my moms. They'd been watching me but they really didn't have shit. They wanted you and they knew that we were close. So if I worked with them, they'd squash all the charges. My moms did some shit a thousand years ago to make the rent and they were gonna give her the backup time for that shit; and the beef for the new charges? The dumb kid that was driving killed himself in the cell and the whole beef for this shit was going to my moms."

"SO YOU DECIDED TO SNITCH ME OUT AND BE A FUCKING NARK!"

"Look, they were gonna get you eventually if you didn't leave the game, and you ain't never gonna leave this shit. Nigga you love it. You're probably one of the smartest most gifted hustlers I've ever seen, but You Can't Beat The Fed's."

"Nigga, Pam is dead because of you!"

"SO WHAT! That bitch wasn't shit she was gonna die anyway, was just a matter of time. I know I don't hear no remorse coming out of you. You? Who has killed, tortured and maimed?"

"Damit Joe we could have beat these cats."

"No, you might have been able to win but the rest of theses cats are just pawns. *You and your "KINGPIN" status.* The only ones who benefit are you and that asshole Ra. And if I know Tino, soon as he figures a way to run this thing without you he's gonna kill Ra if he can. I ain't gonna beg, plead or gravel. I made my decision and I did what I had to do. I know you've made your decision and you'll do what you must. Do what you feel you have too, but because we were friends I ask you to do this one thing for me. Snitch or no snitch, take care of my sister."

"Pam wasn't shit, but the one thing she was, was loyal. When I found out how JB killed her I promised myself that if I found out who the snitch was or if I could kill JB the same way, I would. So today I make good on that promise."

I took the knife that Joe had dropped on the ground and I cut all of his clothes off of him except his draws. Joe was a young

186

man and in fairly good shape so his health would make this a longer process. From this beat-cop that I had on payroll, I was able to get the bullwhip that JB had beaten Pam to death with. Her bloodstains had turned the brown leather a dark burgundy, almost black even. The handle was a long brass tip. It looked like something that a Roman Emperor might have been wearing on a chariot or some shit. Its tips were frayed leather with tiny metal pieces of what looked to be barbed-wire or small razors. This was something that I'm sure JB had handcrafted for the torture of humans. This tool was far too barbaric for the discipline of an animal. I had promised myself the blood of the snitch would mix with hers.

Once again, it was time to make good on that promise.

The first five of six strikes Joe concealed his pain, didn't cry out at all. I knew he was a strong young man but the whip would not allow him to be silent for long. The cracking of that whip was almost louder that the recoil of the rifle. I knew when we went out there that either Joe or I were not coming back. It was killing me on the inside to do what I was doing. Not to mention the physical labor of the job was great. Finally, after sixteen lashes, I stopped. By then Joe was dehydrated, from the screaming and the cold air in his lungs. Quite some time had passed, with him slipping in and out of consciousness several times. Then, the unexpected happened, he spoke.

"Finish it," he uttered in a raspy dry voice. "But do know, you can never leave the game. You will never be able to interact with the public and you will never know normalcy. You will never fully smile; you will never fully enjoy life. Your warmest moment will be a twisted chagrin. Never a belly laugh, just an occasional chuckle. If you could do this to me, because of the rules of the game, your loyalty to the game is greater than your loyalty to self. I betrayed you, yes, to save the lives of my mother and sister. You ask yourself why you did this to me."

Joe was dying and I could tell by the blood he was coughing . He knew he was dying so what he was said he and I both knew would be his last words. He went on to add:

"Pam was just a casually of war, it's not out of loyalty to her that you do this. It's out of loyalty to the title that you covet as your own. But one day you will die and another will carry the title. You could have simply shot me once and I would have been just as dead. But you took this route and this path on purpose.

I was going to kill you out here but I couldn't do it. That little country girl Tammy, you can find her dead under the blankets upstairs. The Fed's wanted me to kill you because they're sick of chasing you. And they know you're gonna disappear soon. So finish what you've started. Because you don't just kill me out here, you kill yourself."

"Very touching, but I've got to tell you that I knew that you had my truck wired for sound straight to the Fed's. That's why I told you we were in North Carolina. We're in Virginia! That's why we never left the house. I didn't want you to know where we were. I could care less about that bitch Tammy. I hate that it ended like this for us kid. But the Feds is right if they think I'm bouncing. This shit has gone way too far and I've seen all I care to."

Two final lashes and the man I knew as Joey Crillz was dead. I stayed out there in those woods for some time. Digging a grave for my friend who had turned snitch. I still remembered him asking me to take care of his sister. I still had those trials and the rest of this shit to deal with. But my footing was sure now. I knew what was going to happen. I got back to the house and Billie was there in the kitchen.

"Where's your friend and how did you get so mush dirt on you?"

"Well it's a long story. You got lunch ready?"

"Yeah, be done by the time you get out of the shower."

"So what you saying? A nigga funky?"

"That's about right."

"Look I know I'm tart. I'm going to the bathroom now to take a long bath so slow your roll on that grub okay?"

"Cool I'll come get you in an hour or so. I need to go the store to get some flour for these biscuits anyway. Can I use your truck?"

" Its cool. Look where is your girl Cammy?"

"That's Tammy, and I don't know. I thought she left with you all earlier. Maybe she went out with your friend."

"You're probably right."

I thought to myself, she went out all right, but it wasn't with Joe."

I heard the truck pull off over the gravel and that was my chance to get Tammy's corpse out of the crib. I dipped into the room that Joe had been sleeping in. I pulled back the blanket and there was no body. All I saw was a large tan envelope. I opened it. Inside were four envelopes all numbered 1,2,3,4. I opened the first one. It was thick. There were several pages of information behind a handwritten letter. The letter instructed me to go to the out-house to consume this information and not speak a word until I got there.

The out-house was old and had not been used for years. The handwriting was Joe's, I would know it anywhere. I remembered it from us sending notes to little shortys in the clubs.

The letter said that if I was reading this, he was probably dead. And dead at my hands. I was stunned, it was like a voice from the grave. He went on to tell me of his snitchery and the reasons why. The letter also told me all that the Fed's knew and what the next few steps to my capture were to be. It also said that he had been assigned to kill me if it looked impossible for them to capture me. The reason that these letters were left was so that I would take care of his sister and know that he loved me as an older brother. The other letters contained information about where his money was stashed and cashiers checks to pay his lawyer's for his mother's defense.

He spoke to me through those letters and I was in a state of sickness. I had so greatly regretted what I had done. Now more than ever before I was sure that this was the end for me and the game. I had committed the most despicable act. I had killed myself. The part of me that wanted any part of the game was gone. Even the fond memories of the so-called good times were somewhat tainted. All the money, gators and furs in the world couldn't make this feeling go away. But still the hustler in me had to continue. Shit, if they had gotten to Joe without my knowledge, who else was down with the FEDS?!

That out-house was already small but now the thing was getting tiny. I started feeling like a rat running in a maze that only lead to death. I wonder why he had me say nothing or had me go to this funky old out-house to ingest this information? Damn!

The house must be bugged, I thought, as well as my truck. That meant the feds had no idea that Joe was dead. Then where did that bitch Tammy go? As these thoughts raced through my mind I could feel the adrenalin moving through me. I'm continued to calculate all the ins and outs.

Shit, I finally figured, That bitch was a Fed! I'm getting out of here. I could take Billie's truck and be gone. I grabbed some essentials, preparing to bounce as fast as I could, but who did I see coming from out front the bank: Billie.

"Hey girl, let me speak to you for a few ticks," I said, grabbing her by the arm.

"Sure what's going on."

"What were you doing in that bank just now?"

"I was closing out my account. Why?"

"Get your ass in this truck now!"

"What's going on? Why are you so upset?"

"Look, you tell me where you know that bitch Cammy from? Now!

"That's Tammy."

"If you don't tell me where you know that bitch from right now I'll splatter your head in this truck, here and now. I ain't bullshit'in."

We were sitting in the back seats of the truck and it was dark so people couldn't really see in. Billie had a valise with her and it was pretty thick. At that moment I had the same 40 cal pistol that I had put up in C.C. right against Billie's head, pressed tightly. This time though, the silencer was attached. So she knew I was serious.

"I love you. I just took all of my money out of the bank from the sale of the properties and I was going to ask you to let me go with you this time when you left. Why are you acting like this?"

I cocked the hammer back. "Bitch-- if you don't tell me where you know that freak Tammy from right now I swear I'll kill you in this truck."

"She'd been working at the restaurant with my cousin. I spoke with her a few times; we hung out and got cool. I remember her saying that she liked Philly niggas so I thought she would be good for your friend. Is something wrong?"

"Yeah... Your answer."

(THOOP-THOOP) Two shots and the chick I'd thought so much of was dead.

I drove off in the truck and never looked back. Later I found out that she had sixty two thousand dollars in the valise. I wasn't sure I made the right move or not. I did know that I never told her where Joe was from. So there was no way she should have known he was from Philly. My gut said fuck it and I followed. All I knew, this bitch could be a Fed too. And I did know this: the Feds don't run out of money or time. They usually have all the bases covered. So to have an agent stay down south and get close to a chick that they suspect might be close to me would be nothing for them. I drove the truck almost all the way home watching every car to see if I was being followed. I watched the sky to see if there were helicopters following me while also wondering if the money was marked. One thing that I did know was that I had to get the dead body of my long time lover turned possible snitch out of this truck. It was her truck. The tags as well as registration were both good, so there was really no reason for the local cops to pull me over.

I stopped at a rest stop on the Jersey Turnpike. It was late. I think about 3:30 am or so, I parked the truck behind a dumpster and began to vacate Billie's body. Although it had been some time, she had not started to smell but rigamortis had set in. She was frozen in position like somebody from the seventies doing the robot. I was hoping that they didn't dump these dumpsters every day. With some other foreign debris, perhaps no one would notice the body.

One Time For The Title

Finally after getting rid of that truck, I was back in NY. I'd taken a few days to get my head together. I stayed out in the Saratoga, a high-rise out in Mount Vernon. My man used to have an apartment in the building. He got killed a few years back and I just kept paying the rent out of habit. It was a place that I never went to; nobody knew about this spot, not even Ra. After I took my shower I took a long look in the mirror. I knew what needed to happen and I now had no problem doing it. I had been away for a minute so know one expected to see me.

I hit Brooklyn, jumped off the D train right at Ocean and Church Ave. Flatbush was pop'in. No different than when I left it. Bustling, moving, I felt that personality that only the streets contain. It's like the streets are an entity of their own not to mention the people. I went to the Menz Club. It didn't seem like it was mine; it was like I was in somebody else's spot. But it's always like that when you bounce. You feel like an outsider for a split second. The reality was that the club was the same but I could care less.

Leek was at the tables doing his thing as usual. He finished his game and came right to the office.

"Yo B, what the fuck s been up with you?"

"Nothin kid, same old thing stack'n and pack'n you know."

"Nigga, you and Ra have pulled off that old jeannie-ass shit. -- as usual. You niggas keep on pullin rabbits out your hats. How the hell yawl keep beating these cases is crazy."

"Leek we got a few cats doing some real time what are you talking about?"

"Man none of the upper players are hurting. Fuck them other cats, they don't matter we can always get some more runners. Fuck'em! They soft. Let'em do the time and we'll mack the dimes."

"So how's *Angie*?"

"She's cool. But she knows what time it is too!"

"Look Leek, do me a favor and get C.C. on the horn; tell her I want to see her right away."

"That's peace I'll hit her right now. Yo, you okay? Seem a little distant?"

"Na, I'm good. You know me, New York State of mind."

In truth, I just wanted to get back to my office to see what the hell was going on. I read a copy of the Post and it had the results of some of the trials, and apparently Mr. A had handled things well in my absence. Our cases were being won. That must have been what the hell Leek was talking about. That was cool, but I wouldn't be happy until I had a talk with Ra.

"Yo B, I've got C.C. on line one."

I picked up the phone. "Hey C. where are you?

"I'm at home do you want me to come there or would you rather come here?"

"Neither. Meet me at the bowling alley in five minutes. You know where, don't you?"

"Sure I'm there in five and I know where."

She met me down behind the alley where the pins are cleaned. C.C. had on some jeans and a leather coat. It was simple but appealing. In my absence it seems that C.C. had taken some of my advice. She was always a little too damn fly with the clothes. She had a good body but she used to go out of her way to show the shit if you ask me. But the stuff she had on at the time was peace. It was like some shit an uptown chick would play. The kind of thing a chick wears when she knows she has a good body and she knows that you know she has a good body but she doesn't have to really go out of her way with the shit.

So Little, But Not Too Late

"C.C., as you know, a lot of things are changing. And I want to know what has changed for you?"

"Well, let me say this, I still love you and I know that you are the one for me. But I don't like the way shit is happening."

"What is it that you see that you don't like?"

"Well, Pam is dead and I don't miss the bitch, but the whole sense of family is kind of gone from this shit. We are respected, feared, envied, hated and loved. But us going on a cruse together is out. These niggas only have one or two things in common now. It wasn't like that before."

"Before what, C.C.?"

"Before you started---"

"Started what? Say it! Tell me what the fuck you think I did to fuck things up."

"You started leaving on these out of town trips and bouncing out on me."

"Wait, first tell me what the things are that you feel the guys in the crew still have in common."

"They either love you, respect you or fear the hell out of you."

"What's wrong with that? There has always been a mixture of emotions when it comes to leadership."

"Yes, but before you where always on the scene and that was needed. It's not going to work without you. And you are making it seem like you don't want to run this shit anymore."

"Where did you get the idea that I'm not going to be on the set running this shit?"

"Like I said when you started splitting all the time."

"Look C.C., this has been a hell of a thing to run and the tolls on the mind and body are great. The more complex the shit is; the more the need for the simplicity of play. You see?"

"Yeah, I hear what you're saying, but that comes with the money and the clout and all the other shit. Nobody said that a break was not needed from time to time but these are some real crucial times and you need to be here. Look, I'm not the only one running this shit, Ra and Tino—"

"I *know* you're not referencing those two clowns; Ra and Tino are running around like Hugh Heffner and Larry Flynt out this bitch. All they want to do is fuck, eat, and kill up some shit. All I hear them talking about is how '*un-fucking*-touchable' they are and we still have JB to deal with."

"Look, I'll handle the shit. Just give me a few days to sort shit out and get with Agronsky and all will be cool. Damn!"

"Yo, I know that you have a lot on your mind so let me make this easy for you. I will stop by the club later and see how you are making out."

C.C bounced and to tell the truth I was glad that she said that she would be back later. I wanted someone to talk to but not necessarily about the game. Actually I think what I need was some one to talk to who had no idea about the shit. I began to wonder what Nicky was up to.

"Yo Nicky how are you?

"I'm fine. You Okay?"

"Yeah, I'm cool."

"You don't sound cool. You sound like you have a lot on your mind. As well you should. I haven't heard from you in quite a few '*ticks*' as you say."

"Look Nick—I've been…"

"Oh, I know what you've been; you've been running a major criminal organization. The shit's only on the news almost every night. I thought you had a little crew that was making some smart moves and a little money not the fucking black Mafia. Your shit is all over the place!"

"Nicky, I told you that I was soon to be done with the shit. And since I told you that, so much has happened that I have no doubt that I want this life to be a memory."

"Well that's all fine and well but I can't have anything to do with this."

"Oh, so let me get this right, as long as my shit was some small potatoes it was tolerable. You find out that there's some real money happening and you want to leave me alone."

"No, not some real money, some real chance of me getting killed or maybe worse."

"My God - - you're acting just like Ra said!"

"Are you talking about that psychopath that you're life long friends with? Who's running around committing sadistic crimes that you are permitting? And you think I care what he says about me?"

"For starters, Ra doesn't work for me he is grown and does what he wants. I can't control him anymore than you can."

"Yes, I hear you speaking; I've also seen you and him together and I can tell that if you didn't want something to happen he would stop or at least take the edge off of his evil ways."

"Well, you've been doing your homework now haven't you?"

"What homework? It's all over the street and on half of the news. And when I say *or worse* I mean this: my friend at the coroner's office says that he's seen the bodies of some of Ra's victims and they want to study his brain for medical science."

"That's enough. I don't want you discussing your thoughts about Ra with me anymore. Are you with me or not?"

"I have two degrees from Maryland University, one in Accounting and one in Finance. I have completed the Johns Hopkins Leadership and Development Program and I now have accomplished my MBA from Johns Hopkins. I have not made all of these sacrifices just to get killed at a stop light by a bullet that was meant for someone else."

At this point, she was really starting to work my nerves.

"If you think I'm impressed with the school shit I'm not. The accomplishments are cool and all but what does your scholastic resume have to do with me? We all make sacrifices. Again, are you with me or not?"

"I'm not sure I just…"

"Let me make this easy for you. I have a gift for you, hold on…" When I put her on hold that was what I also did with that whole line of thinking. Put it all on hold.

I knew then and there I'd never speak to Nicky again.

I paged Ra but didn't hear back from him. The funny thing was I didn't worry or feel that same urgent concern that I once did. I knew he had gotten my pages but was probably just fucking. So my evening went on. I thought about it and after about twenty minutes I called C.C.

"Yo, I need to talk to you. Meet me at the bodega in forty minutes." Before she could respond I hung up.

She arrived and I asked her to come with me. She asked me if she needed to bring anything with her. At first, I told her no. Then I paused, and told her to get what she needed. I'd forgotten that C.C. had been promoted and was not on the same status anymore. The something that she went back in the store for was some heat.

"Are you good?" I asked her.

"As s good as it gets," she replied.

I asked her to drive and to take me to her place so we could talk.

She was unusually calm and seemed to be sure of what she was doing but not anxious. We pulled up to her building and parked my car. I got out and so did she.

I started trying to flag a cab.

"What are you doing?" she asked.

"I'm flagging a cab to go to your place."

"But this is my place."

"Na—no it's not. I didn't mean the place that we've provided for you. I want to go to *your* place. The spot that you've always kept just in case this shit goes away. The place where you feel the most secure. And yo, you take me to your mom's place and I'll spank your ass."

"You think you know everything don't you?

"Na, I just know you better than you think I do."

"Why are you flagging a cab we could just take your car?"

"You never know who could be watching out for my whip, but a cab is always anonymous."

"Always thinking! I'll give you that."

The cab came and we had quite a ride to get to her place. I knew C.C. was the type to have her own little place. I was actually quite curious to se what her place would look like. It had been a long time since that other incident at her other place. As we got to her elevator, she told me she never kept much food there because at times she wasn't around for weeks on end. I asked her how long she'd had this loft. About a year or so, she said.

She put some music on and I just chilled for a few. Truth be told, I really wanted to go to sleep. Not that I was sleepy, I just yearned for the peace and serenity that sleep brought. When I got there it was light out, when I opened my eyes I could tell it was dark outside. I also smelled some food cooking. There was a glass of wine in front of me and I felt rested for the most part.

"Yo, C.C.! Where are you?

"I'm over here"

Her place was big, I mean real big. It was like an indoor garage. But she had these little wall like things up all over the place I could see two of her motorcycles parked and an

old Cadi convertible. The shit was mint.

I asked her how long had I been there?

"About three hours. I was going to wake you up when I came out the bathroom, but you seemed like you needed the sleep. I had to go and get some grub anyway."

"Yo, tell me exactly what the hell's been happening lately!"

"Well mostly the same as always. The club is making good doe and the crew is functioning but it's just on cruse control. That lawyer of yours is no joke, he's winning a lot of small shit but some of the pee-wee leaguers are getting little bids. I have a friend on the inside who says no one's talking. But the ones who are getting time don't know shit anyway. Ra and Tino are the ones fucking shit up. They're not giving the orders, they're just letting shit happen. They do spend a lot of time following JB but it don't take two to get that job done. Oh, and they still do the money pick-ups. The other problem is Tino thinks he's some kind of Gunga-Din or something. When he does give the word for shit to happen, he talks to them shorties like they ain't shit. I tried to tell him that a young killer or an inexperienced killer is still a killer. He told me to stay out of it, so I let it be."

"Okay. What are you doing while all of this is going on?"

"Well besides watching the club, moving my part of product and handling debt collections, I have a lot on my plate. Not to mention I'm picking up on all the work that Pam was doing with those girls she had. It's actually a pretty good turnover of money now that I see what was happening. I give her credit, she was putting in work."

"What? From 'she ain't shit and ain't doing shit' to 'I give her a lot of credit'? That's quite a shift."

"Well Pam still wasn't my favorite person, but I will say she was doing more than it looked like."

"Now if you really want to shock me tell me you miss her."

"That shit is not going to happen. How's the food?"

"Good grub, I'll give you that. What's the *pool man* up to?"

"He helps with the girls when he can, but I still say he spends too much time playing with the chicks. But he's a man and they are all gonna do that."

The convo went on for a while but it slowly started to take on a very friendly atmosphere. We started looking at each other and for the first time, I think I really felt something for C.C. She looked directly in my eyes most of the time. It was as though she had a real concern for what I was saying and for me as well.

For some reason I really wanted to fuck this chick. After Nicky had acted an ass earlier; I think I just wanted some good pussy to fall into. It was weird, but I still had thoughts of Billie in my head. But fuck her, I thought. Cool or no cool, she was a Fed who was gonna send me inside, at least that's what I allowed myself to believe. If that's the case she got exactly what she would have done to me. Plus C.C.'s tits were looking good from where I was sitting. At that moment I felt like I'd been living with discipline just a little bit too long. I planned on having me some good old reckless fun tonight.

I've gotta say the whole thing to me went down in slow motion. (Well, some parts were in slow motion). I asked C.C. to come and sit beside me.

"Brisco sweetheart, I know you have a lot on your mind let me help you clear you head," she whispered while coming over to me.

And clear my head she did.

After a long and very physical evening, combined with tender moments, I awoke in the back seat of the Cadi. With C.C. wrapped in my muscular arms and I in hers. I got out the car undetected by her. The evening was like a blur that I could only describe as many joyful events. Everywhere I looked showed the evidence of our joy. Used condoms in the shower, on the floor of the Cadi, on the couch, where I remember things getting kicked off at. Bottles of Moe all over. Some unfinished, some upside down and empty. It looked like several couples had sex in this place. I now knew how C.C was able to get some of those cats to pay up their debts. The pussy was the shit, though I'd never let her know it. As she awoke I was in the shower trying to figure my next move. She had breakfast going, pancakes and the whole nine. As our eyes met across the breakfast table she looked me in the eye with a sweet glance.

"Thank You," she simply said.

That was about the most feminine I'd ever seen C.C. act the whole time I'd known her. I wondered if I should roll or stay. Fuck it, I thought, I'm staying. Ended up staying there for two weeks, fucking C.C and getting to know another side of her. Still handling business of course, but coming back to her crib to chill, eat and fuck. I mean what the hell, the ass was excellent and at this point I could care less about the rank structure. Maybe I was slipp'in, but my head felt clear and I seemed to find focus once again.

In my mind I was able to plot the entire course that I needed. I decided that JB had to die that night. Fuck whatever Ra and

Tino had going, this motherfucker killed Pam and his ass was dead tonight.

I meet Ra at the club.

"Peace god"

"Peace"

"What's up "

"Look, JB dies tonight. Do you want in?"

"You know I want in, but we've been tailing this guy for-"

"Yeah, for months and he's still breathing. This motherfucker dies tonight. You in or out? The reports are that you and Tino have been handling shit swell. I never thought anything less would go down, but this asshole dies tonight. I know where he stays and I'll send some young cats to spray his place and you and I will catch him coming out and that's it."

"Why do you want to get your hands dirty with this shit god? We can let that kid *young bitch* do the work. He ain't doing shit else."

"Look Ra, there's no time to teach the kid. I can handle the shit myself if you don't want to come along."

"NO I WANT THE KID TO DO IT HOW ABOUT THAT!"

"All right then, it's settled. The kid will do it but tell me why Ra. Why not Tino or one of the others?"

"Because that kid is running around with our clout but he ain't really put no real work in for it. So he sold some crack and dope? So what he's been around it. He pushed a little blow and some weed to his friends. He hasn't ever really **earned** the title he's strolling around Brooklyn with. I for one think it's time the prick did some fucking work."

"True indeed, the kid's resume is not as long as some. You want him to earn some stripes fine; but Tino hasn't done shit since he's been back either. I say we let the two of them handle this shit together and call it a day. But Ra, this shit needs to be neat and tonight. Agreed."

"True indeed god."

"Yo Ra, I want your bond on it."

"You got it god, word is bond JB dies tonight."

I knew what was gonna happen and I had no intention of getting involved in it. I could see that Ra wanted Ace dead so Tino could get a formal bump up. I could care less at this point. Tino was my man too, to a certain extent. But, I wondered, in the game how cool are you really with anybody? When the club closed and the music stopped so did all that nightclub love. I'd grown sick of it. Let them kill the kid if that's what it came down to. It was anybody's play at this point. Long as I knew what the fuck I needed to do.

I told C.C. to meet me at her place.

She was there and I was shocked that so much of her shit was gone when I got there.

"What happened to the old school Cadi and the bikes and shit?"

"It's time to let those things go, don't you think."

"Yeah but I thought you loved them Jet skis and all that shit?"

"I did, but there's things I love more than things. Plus I have a gift for you."

"Oh yeah? What?"

"I'll show you later."

I called the kid and told him to meet me a certain address, 611 Ocean Ave. in Flatbush. I told the kid I'd be upstairs but he would have to ask to speak to Darren Dunn. He'd then be patted down. He was also informed of the situation that was to go on later that night.

He entered the room and I told him that his ass had better listen, closer than he'd ever listened before. I told him that this convo would guide his life. We talked for about two hours, I discussed with him the regrets that the game had given me. I also told him what he needed to know to continue with any level of success. I didn't waste my time trying to tell him to quit the game, for he'd already come too far and lost too much. Not to mention the fact that he loved the shit the same way that I had early on. I gave him the keys to my condo in the Saratoga. I told him that it was a promotion. I then instructed him to get some sleep because tonight he would define his life, his existence as a top player or his being considered a bum forever.

We met at 2:00am and I could see that everyone was ready. Tino had that same cunning greedy silly-ass look that he always had. To Ra it was just another body to put in the ground, but I knew he felt something different was up. I knew him like I knew myself. I saw past the gruff exterior and I knew this nigga could tell I was up to some shit. The kid's ass was in a ball. He looked like a pitbull just before the fight, ready but still pensive.

"Look, ain't no amateurs out this bitch. Go in there and handle your motherfucking business. Take no prisoners. I want everything in the motherfucker dead. You hear me. If this clown has gold fish you take them out the bowl, pour salt on them then stomp them. Do you hear me! I want everything in there dead. JB killed one of ours don't forget that, this shit is way past personal. Anybody got any questions?"

Some fool had the nerve to say yes. I shot him right there.

"Any more questions?? There's only one way out of this."

I could see what I'd done got the crew on some real shit. If they were not already focused, they were now.

212

To be honest, I had to muster my shit together for this. I was sure that this was for all the chips. Any weakness at this point and I could be next.

We got to JB's, I signaled the young ones to get into position. I had Ra confirm that JB was in there. He signaled me that it was on. The young cats then charged JB's backdoor. Me and Ra chilled. Tino was in the crew with the young cats. Ace was with them too. I heard a lot of gunfire. Mostly small caliber shots. I' knew that most of that was the youngsters. Then a short silence and more shots.

Out of nowhere a loud shot gun blast.

One barrel and the other. A body staggered out the back door still on his feet but obviously dying. Ra gestured to wait before shooting. The cat fell to his knees. He remained on his knees as Ra ran towards him. It was Tino. His left ankle blown damn-near off. How he even walked was amazing. His whole back was more of his front than anything else. He struggled to speak but the words did come. He told us JB was still in there. His raspy voice took me back to Joe in those woods for just a split second. He looked up at Ra.

"JB's still alive."

"Did JB do this to you?" inquired Ra.

"Na, it was the kid. Yo, he's better than you thought, you know. Too good to be from the hood."

Just that moment, Tino Bailey expired.

Ra looked at me, stunned. "Too good to be from the hood."

There was still some shooting going on but not nearly as many guns.

Ra and I both looked at each other, needing not to say a word, for we both knew. I ran in first and Ra gave me cover. I had no idea how the place was laid out. I just kept shooting to keep the fire off me. Ra had my back and I was sure of that. I saw JB, he was bent over, I thought he'd been hit. I shot at him and missed. Tell you what, if that old man had been hit and still moved that fast I could only imagine how fast he was before. The shots slowed and the only people in the place was JB, Ra, myself and the kid. I heard a slap and a gun hit the floor. Then I heard a quick scuffle and the sounds of bones cracking. It was Ra. He had Ace, his hand was behind the kids back and the other hand was around the kids neck.

"Say it. You piece of dry dog shit say it!"

"I don't know what you're talking about Ra!"

"Say you don't know what I'm talking about one more time and I'll snap your neck like a pretzel. You greedy little shit; you wanted Tino dead so you could get more juice. You probably had plans of trying to bump me off in this shit too. Now you tell your *hero* over there that you shot Tino in the back like a bitch. So I can go ahead and kill you."

"I never wanted"

"Say it or your ass will die now."

The grip Ra had on his neck was so tight that the words could barley get escape out the kids throat. Ra's arms were powerful, no way the kid could overcome his grip. And with one arm broken badly, the kid was toast. It was more pain than he could tolerate.

"Okay I shot Tino."

"Tell him the rest," insisted Ra.

"Common man, my throat. Ra, I hate your ass take this…" (BRANT, BRANT, umph, BRANT)

"Ooo you nasty little bitch," screamed Ra.

"Ra what's up?" I yelled out.

"This bitch shitted on himself, ho ass kid. I should break your other arm."

"Yea go ahead. Finally I got your ass Ra. I shitted on you"

"Tell it you Ho!"

"I --- I"— crack---Bloom! Bloom!

Two shotgun blast's went off I saw the kid take a full charge to the chest.

Ra went out the balcony window. I don't know if the blast pushed him out or he jumped. But he was gone. I spun around and fired. It was JB. He'd made it to his feet and I had shot him dead. The shot went straight to his head. My hollow points blew his head almost off his shoulders. He was dead for sure. I saw his corpus and gave him one more blast to the heart to make sure he was toast.

I ran over to the balcony were Ra had been standing. I looked down and saw nothing but bare street. I also heard sirens coming. I ran to the top of the building and jetted over a few rooftops. I went down a fire escape and I was ghost. No looking back; I knew the cops would soon be everywhere.

I dared not use my celly. I called C.C. and told her to come and get me from this little pool hall. It was an out the way rinky-dink spot that no one would ever expect to see me in. I was surprised she got there so quickly. I asked her what was up with the new whip she pulled up in.

"This was the surprise that I had for you."

It was a slick old school convertible.

I told her it was hot, but I needed something low key.

"Yes but you won't always need to be low key."

I took C.C. out to my townhouse. She had never been there before and had no idea that I had such a place. We chilled and got some sleep. When the morning came I was still undecided about whether I wanted to tell C.C. my plan. My life had been a series of secrets and shadows, to begin to let some one in was more that difficult. Plus, I had Ra on my mind. I was not sure if he was hit and bleeding, dead, or alive. Knowing him he could have done one of his infamous back flips and made the leap with no problem, or perhaps not. Maybe the cops caught him a few blocks away? Maybe not? One thing I knew was that I didn't have time to continue dwelling on what may or may not have happened to him. My head was filled with what exactly would happen to me in the near future.

No matter my plight, I couldn't help thinking about Bleed, and how much love I had for the kid. But shit, I thought, his ass killed Tino in fine fashion. I still hadn't figured out what Tino was really trying to say about being too good to be from the hood. Was the kid a plant put in by the FEDS? Na, couldn't be. If he was sent by them they could long ago have busted me when the kid found out about the control room, or when the chick got it in the boiler room. Was he working for JB? Or connected with someone else? Fuck it, I reasoned, he's dead now no matter who he *was* working for.

Hit The Road

Without warning, I'd been blindsided by the unthinkable: My situation got hot. To escape the heat I'd be forced to split town, on the spot, a one-way trip to destination figure-it-out-on-the-fly. Sure I had cash and an assortment of other assets I'd acquired from a healthy life in the game; but what good were the items now when I had no time or means to access them? I've still got a grip, but it won't last forever.

I needed to make two phone calls. One was to a childhood friend who was in D.C. A kid I always spoke to every few years, Steve Rimpsy aka "Remy." Remy always kept a job, I thought he drove a bus or something. Maybe not a good job, but pretty consistent bread, just the thing I'd need for the short term. I thought maybe he'd be able to hook me up with something at his gig. A ten minute conversation told me he was glad to hear from me but that the jobs he worked at required a clean record.

The second call went to Keith Tillman. Damn! He wound up saying the same shit Remy had said about his hands being tied. Plus that cat was all the way out in Cali somewhere. So what the fuck was I to do? I couldn't get a job. I couldn't stay in this town. I couldn't use my real identity. Simply put, I was fucked! Plus there was the chick C.C. I wasn't sure if I wanted her in on this shit or not. On the one hand, she could be a help. But if she started acting simple and shit she could turn out to be a major problem.

I told C.C. that I was glad things went down like they did with us that I wanted to make her dinner. She took a bath and we quickly made love. Not sexin not fuckin we made love. I needed the warm touch of a female to remind me of what life was about. And to take the feeling of death off of my mind. As she rested I made dinner, eventually calling her to the table. She told me this was the happiest time of her life. She asked me why I wasn't eating, I told her I was concerned about Ra and that I wasn't comfortable eating. This was part lie, mostly truth.

I wanted to give her something, something that I knew she always wanted. So I did.

"Look C.C. you've always had a real curious nature and I know there's a lot about me you want to know. So tonight at this moment, I grant you three questions, only one of which I will answer completely."

"So what are you my genie in a bottle?" responded C.C. in typical fashion.

"Just ask the questions."

"Okay. First, who made this food, it's really good.

"That's one."

"No, that's not one of my questions. Come on now. Okay, here's my three questions:

How much money is there in this?

How many people have you killed?

Do you feel anything for me?"

I paused and told her, "I'm glad you're enjoying the food."

"What about my answers? I'm anxious to know."

"Let me talk to you for a few ticks. How long have you had these curiosities?"

"For a while, but I figured I'd find out in due time if it was meant for me to know. You said you would only answer one so I'm good with whichever one you answer."

"Well you know I'm not telling you about the dough. That's out. I don't even know why you wasted a question with that shit."

She suddenly started coughing, rather intensely.

"Are you all right?" I asked.

She said that some food had gone down the wrong pipe, but she was cool.

I then told her that the number of people I had killed was six—but including her the count was now at seven.

"What do you mean, with me it's seven?"

"C.C. dear, I can't take you with me. My next trip has to be a solo mission. And that food you just ate was poisoned."

At that moment she started convulsing and gagging profusely. She spit some blood, not much but enough for me to see she was dying. Her robe flew open and I saw her heaving young breast bounce and shake. I watched her eyes roll back into her head, but that last look that she could control was of such disbelief and fear. She reached her hand out to me as if to ask for assistance. It was not a reach of attack, like one might think. It was as if she wanted just to stay with me a few seconds longer. I lowered my head and whispering softly: "I love you C.C., as much as I can love…which isn't very much."

I stayed there about five minutes or so. I wrapped her body, cleaned up the blood and did away with corpse. I was headed out, all ends were clear. The crew that I'd started with Ra was now over, the leftovers now there for the taking. I'd no choice but to let the other young cats have this game, for I had outlived my competition and my era. There would always be young cats trying to be The One, The Top Boss, The Big Baller, or whatever the next term would inevitably be. But for the rest of my life, I would have to live far beneath the radar of the bright lights and the glitz. A warm leather not a flowing mink, a bus-pass not an electronic remote start for my "butta whip". I would likely find myself in all the places you would never find an individual of my *accomplishment*. I'd be lucky if I landed some sort of job somewhere like Remy, driving a bus or something. Answering to some boot licking moron, who'd never made or seen a couple hundred grand his whole life. For now, I had to embrace humility and it would be my prison. This was but part of the price of my flamboyance and grand living. But what would I tell the next woman I really liked or loved? What would I put on my resume as my former job? Who would be cited as my references? Certainly not the corpses. And how would I fill the gaps in my employment history which span a lifetime?

I knew exactly what I'd do: I would tell them that after all these years and all I've learned; I'm still but a thirsty hustler from the projects.

I, KINGPIN